THE PENNILESS PEER

Lovely, red-haired Fenella Lambert had loved her handsome cousin since they had played together as children. So when Lord Perequine Corbury returned from fighting Napoleon's armies to find himself destitute, it was she who suggested the daring plan that would regain his fortune—even though it meant his marriage to another. With Perequine, Fenella embarked on a perilous adventure that brought her closer to danger than she had ever been before.

The captivating new novel by
today's best-loved writer of romantic fiction,
Barbara Cartland

Books by BARBARA CARTLAND

Romantic Novels

The Fire of Love
The Unpredictable Bride
Love Holds the Cards
A Virgin in Paris
Love to the Rescue
Love Is Contraband
The Enchanting Evil
The Unknown Heart
The Secret Fear
The Reluctant Bride
The Pretty Horse-Breakers
The Audacious Adventuress

Lost Enchantment
Halo for the Devil
The Irresistible Buck
The Complacent Wife
The Odious Duke
The Daring Deception
No Darkness for Love
The Little Adventure
Lessons in Love
Journey to Paradise
The Bored Bridegroom
The Penniless Peer

Autobiographical and Biographical

The Isthmus Years 1919–1939
The Years of Opportunity 1939–1945
I Search for Rainbows 1945–1966
We Danced All Night 1919–1929
Ronald Cartland
    (with a Foreword by Sir Winston Churchill)
Polly, My Wonderful Mother

Historical

Bewitching Women
The Outrageous Queen
    (The Story of Queen Christina of Sweden)
The Scandalous Life of King Carol
The Private Life of King Charles II
The Private Life of Elizabeth, Empress of Austria
Josephine, Empress of France
Diane de Poitiers
Metternich—the Passionate Diplomat

Sociology

You in the Home
The Fascinating Forties
Marriage for Moderns
Be Vivid, Be Vital
Love, Life and Sex
Look Lovely, Be Lovely
Vitamins for Vitality
Husbands and Wives

Etiquette
The Many Facets of Love
Sex and the Teenager
The Book of Charm
Living Together
Woman—The Enigma
The Youth Secret
The Magic of Honey

        Barbara Cartland's Health Food Cookery Book
        Barbara Cartland's Book of Beauty and Health
        Men Are Wonderful

The Penniless Peer

Barbara Cartland

THE PENNILESS PEER
A Bantam Book published June 1974

Library of Congress Cataloging in Publication Data

Cartland, Barbara, 1902–
   The penniless peer.

   I. Title.
[PZ3.C247Pe] [PR6005.A765] 823'.9'12 74-5058

PRINTED IN THE UNITED STATES OF AMERICA

The Penniless Peer

Chapter One

1817

"Kiss me, Hetty, kiss me again!"

"No ... Periquine ... I ought to go."

"You cannot go—you must stay with me! I have been waiting for so long to see you alone."

There was silence while Lord Corbury kissed Hetty so passionately that she could hardly breathe.

"Dear Periquine," she murmured after a moment, "I love you when you kiss me like that."

"And I love you," he said in his deep voice. "When are you going to marry me, my darling?"

"Oh Periquine!"

He loosened his hold on her for a moment and looked down at her face. It was a very lovely face and it had been acclaimed by all London.

Very fair, with large misty blue eyes, Hetty Baldwyn had been the toast of St. James's from the moment she appeared on the social scene.

Now after two seasons she was an unrivalled beauty, the "Incomparable" who was pursued not only by the Bucks and Dandies of the *Beau Monde*, but by all the other young men who wished to be in the fashion.

"What do you mean, 'Oh Periquine!'?" Lord Corbury asked.

Hetty laid her cheek against his shoulder.

1

"You know Papa would not allow it."

"Damn it all, why should we trouble ourselves with your father?" Lord Corbury enquired. "We will run away, Hetty. We will be married, and then there is nothing he can do about it."

He stopped speaking because Hetty was looking at him in wide eyed surprise.

"You mean go to . . . Gretna Green?" she enquired in shocked tones.

"Why not?" he asked roughly. "Once we are over the border and married, there is little your father can do except berate us, and who cares about that?"

Hetty pouted her red lips and looked more alluring than ever.

"But Periquine, I want a big wedding with bridesmaids and all my friends there. I have planned my gown already, and I want to wear Mama's diamond tiara."

She saw a dark and ominous look in Lord Corbury's eyes and added hastily:

"Of course you would make a most alluring and handsome bridegroom!"

"What the devil does it matter how or where we are married as long as we are?" Lord Corbury enquired. "Bridesmaids, spectators, they are all of no importance! What matters is us, Hetty! You will be my wife and then no-one can take you from me."

"It would be wonderful," Hetty breathed softly. "At the same time Periquine, I would not wish to upset Papa. He is proud of me and it would break his heart if I did anything so shameful as running away to Gretna Green."

"Then what are we to do?" Lord Corbury asked despondently.

He was an exceedingly good looking young man, tall with broad shoulders, and features which caused a flutter in the heart of every maiden on whom he cast his grey eyes.

He also had a slightly raffish air about him which even the fastidious Hetty found irresistible.

She disengaged herself now from his arms and

stood looking up at him, her riding-habit of turquoise blue velvet revealing the exquisite curves of her slight figure.

She had taken off her hat with its gauze veil when she had entered the room, and the sun coming through the diamond-paned casement-windows seemed to halo the pale gold of her hair and gave her an ethereal beauty which made Lord Corbury gaze at her as if spell-bound.

"I love you, Hetty," he said unsteadily, "I cannot live without you."

"And I love you, Periquine," she replied, "but we must be careful, very careful. I have not told Papa that you are home; so he has no idea that we are together at the moment."

"Then what is your excuse for being here?" Lord Corbury asked.

"I told Papa I was riding to the Priory to call on your House-keeper, Mrs. Buckle, who is ill. He commended me on being so thoughtful."

"He is certain to learn sooner or later that I am back," Lord Corbury said sulkily.

"I have thought of that," Hetty replied. "I shall tell him that Mrs. Buckle expects you any day. If one is going to lie, one should always tell a good one."

"And do you think I enjoy all these lies and subterfuges?" Lord Corbury asked.

"What else can we do?" Hetty asked.

"You can marry me!" he answered sharply.

"And what would we live on?" she enquired.

"We could live here."

He looked round the room as he spoke, noting for the first time that, while the wood panelling was old and beautiful, the rest of the furnishings were threadbare and needed renewing.

The fringe was falling away from the velvet curtains, the pattern had almost disappeared from the once valuable Persian carpet, several of the chairs needed repairing, and it was easy to see there were places on the walls where pictures had once hung.

Hetty followed his gaze.

"I know you love your home, Periquine," she said, "but it would cost thousands of pounds, really thousands, to put it in order and make it habitable."

"And I have not even a thousand pence," Lord Corbury said bitterly.

"I know, I know," Hetty said, "and that is why it would be quite useless for you to speak to Papa or even to hint that you wish to marry me. He is determined that I shall make a brilliant marriage. At the moment he favours Sir Nicolas Waringham."

"Waringham!" Lord Corbury ejaculated furiously. "Do you think you would be happy with that stuck-up, stiff-necked snob, who is far too conscious of his own consequence?"

"He is very very wealthy," Hetty said softly.

"While I am penniless!" Lord Corbury exclaimed. "A penniless Peer! That is a joke, is it not?"

Hetty appeared to shiver.

"I must go, Periquine, I dare not stay here talking to you, but I will try to come over tomorrow. I will tell Papa Mrs. Buckle is still poorly, that I have promised to take her some nourishing soup. Mama will approve of that too, she is always saying I do not pay enough attention to the sick and poor."

"Then pay attention to me!" Lord Corbury demanded, taking her into his arms and lifting her chin to look down at her blue eyes. "You are so lovely, so incredibly, unbelievably lovely!"

His lips were on hers and as he felt her respond to his passion, he drew her closer and closer still.

There was no doubt he aroused an emotion in the beautiful Hetty which few other men were able to do.

She was considered rather cold by the majority of her admirers, but now her lips quivered beneath Lord Corbury's and her arms crept round his neck.

When finally he raised his head, her eyes were warm with passion and her breasts were moving tumultuously beneath her velvet jacket.

"I love you! I love you," he cried. "God, how I love you!"

He would have kissed her again, but she put out her hands to stop him.

"No, Periquine, I must go, it is getting late. We must not arouse any suspicion, or it will be impossible for us to meet again."

She turned towards the door as she spoke, and when he would have followed her she warned him:

"Do not come with me. My groom must not see you."

"You will come tomorrow?" Lord Corbury pleaded.

"If it is possible," Hetty promised. "But Sir Nicolas is arriving to stay with us and Papa will expect me to amuse him."

"Curse Waringham! Why should he have so much money, when my pockets are to let?"

"That is the question I have already asked myself," Hetty answered. "Periquine, I promise you things would be very different if only you were rich."

She gave him a provocative glance from under her long eye lashes and added:

"Can you not make some money somehow? If you had only a small fortune, I am sure Papa would look favourably upon you. After all, yours is an ancient title."

"As old as the Priory," Lord Corbury replied, "and in the same rotten state of disrepair."

His voice was bitter again. Hetty turned back to stand on tip-toe and plant a soft kiss on his cheek before she went across the room as lightly as a butterfly.

She opened the door, made a graceful gesture with her hand that she knew herself was very alluring and then disappeared, leaving Lord Corbury with an impression of beguiling blue eyes and smiling red lips.

He stood for a moment staring at the door when it shut behind her as if he expected her to return, and then he walked gloomily to the window to stand looking out at the unkept lawns, the broken sundial, the flower-beds which were a mass of weeds, and the

balustrade edging the terrace which was overgrown
with moss.

As he stood still deep in his thoughts, unexpectedly he heard a sound behind him. There was a faint
click and then a slight scrape of something being
moved.

He turned round. A part of the panelling beside
the fireplace was opening and as he watched it, a
small face peered round the room. Lord Corbury saw
two very large enquiring eyes, below an oval forehead
and a head of very deep red hair which curled in
untidy profusion.

Lord Corbury stared.

"Fenella!" he ejaculated and walked to the open
panel.

The newcomer gave a kind of squeak of surprise at seeing him. Putting out his hand he took her
by the arm and dragged her into the room, shaking
her.

"What are you doing here, Fenella?" he stormed.
"How dare you hide in the Priest's Hole! Your behaviour is intolerable! I have a very good mind to give
you a good spanking!"

She swayed backwards and forwards with the
fury of his shaking and at the same time her eyes
laughed up at him:

"No, no! Periquine!" she cried. "Last time you
spanked me it hurt abominably! And anyway I am
now too old."

He released his hold on her.

"What do you mean 'too old'?"

"I am eighteen. Had you forgotten?"

"Good God, it's not possible!" he exclaimed. "You
were only a child when I went away."

"Nonsense!" she retorted. "I was nearly fifteen,
but I looked younger. Now I am a grown-up young
lady!"

"You certainly do not look or behave like one,"
he answered.

It was true she was very small and her head

barely reached his shoulder. He might be excused for thinking she was very much younger than her age.

She wore a cotton frock which she had long ago out-grown, and it clung to her body revealing the new maturity of her small breasts.

It had lost its colour through frequent washing, but nevertheless it could not disguise the perfection of her figure or the fact that her hair caught in the sunshine had fiery lights which looked like tiny tongues of flame.

Her eyes seemed over-large for her face. Their colour was the strange green of the pools in the wood, and they had the same clarity as the streams which glittered and glimmered in the sunshine seeping through the branches of the trees.

She was not classically beautiful like Hetty, but she had a kind of elfin loveliness which was irresistible. Her lips curved upwards at the corners and her eyes seemed to dance with laughter.

Her skin was white except that on her small slightly tip-tilted nose there were a number of freckles.

"Eighteen!" Lord Corbury exclaimed, "and still getting into mischief! Perhaps you will explain to me what the hell you are doing in the Priest's Hole eavesdropping on my conversation."

"It was very edifying!" Fenella said with a mischievous glance.

He put out his hand as if to take hold of her shoulder and shake her again, but she slipped quickly out of his reach.

"I could not help it, Periquine! I could not really!" she explained. "I heard you coming and there was nothing I could do but hide myself. I knew Hetty would not be pleased to see me."

"Why ever not?" Lord Corbury enquired.

"Hetty does not much like other women," Fenella replied, "especially when she has a romantic assignation with a handsome Beau!"

She looked at Lord Corbury as she spoke, noting the intricate folds of his white cravat, his exquisitely cut coat, and tight yellow pantaloons.

"You do look smart, Periquine! I thought you were irresistible in your uniform, but now you are a perfect Adonis."

"I wish to God I were back in the Army," Lord Corbury snapped. "At least I had something else to occupy my mind besides lack of money."

"I was afraid you would be upset when you learnt what was happening on the estate," Fenella said sympathetically.

She perched herself as she spoke on the arm of a sofa.

"Why did not somebody tell me?" Lord Corbury enquired.

"I did think of writing to you," Fenella replied, "but what good would it have done? You were in France, and even if you had received my letter, which I doubted, there was little that could be altered until you returned."

"And what do you imagine I can do now?" Lord Corbury asked aggressively. "Swayer came to see me in London the day before yesterday and informed me that I could not let the farms unless they are first repaired, and that I could not repair them because I had no money! How could things have got into such a state?"

"Your father was very ill before he died," Fenella said quietly, "and things just went from bad to worse. MacDonald gave up his farm, and Grimble refused to continue unless the barns were repaired, and naturally no-one would rent them in the state they are in now."

She paused and added almost reluctantly:

"The other farms have been without tenants for nearly three years."

"I asked Swayer why he did not write to me," Lord Corbury said, "and he said it was not his business."

"I suppose that Johnson, your father's agent, should have done so," Fenella said. "But he was always a surly and difficult man, and he was so incensed when he received no salary for six months that he just packed up and went. He did not even say goodbye."

"Empty farms! No rents coming in and the house collapsing over my head!" Lord Corbury exclaimed. "I have seen the holes in the roof, I have seen how many ceilings there are down."

"The ceiling in the Picture Gallery is the only one that really matters," Fenella said.

"Picture Gallery!" Lord Corbury scoffed. "Why should that matter? There are no pictures there. They have all gone years ago."

"They had to sell the last Van Dyke so that your father could have a few luxuries in the six months before he died," Fenella said. "I believe they obtained quite a reasonable price for it, but there was already so much owing, so many debts unpaid, so many wages overdue, I am afraid there will be nothing left."

"There *is* nothing left."

"Oh Periquine, I am so sorry! I have been so looking forward to your coming home. I have thought about it and longed to see you, and now everything is spoilt."

"You can hardly expect me to be jubilant," Lord Corbury said sourly.

"No, of course not," Fenella agreed. "And you also want to . . . marry . . . Hetty?"

It was a question spoken in a soft nervous voice.

"Of course I want to marry her!" Lord Corbury replied. "She is the most beautiful girl I have ever seen! And she loves me, Fenella, I know she loves me. We could run away together if it were not for that pompous and snobbish old father of hers."

"Sir Virgil is very proud of his daughter," Fenella said as if she were finding an excuse for him.

"I should be proud of her too, if she were my wife," Lord Corbury said. "What the hell am I to do, Fenella?"

He walked back to the window as he spoke, and Fenella watching him realised it was just like old times.

There were six years between them in age, and

yet, because they were second cousins and lived within half a mile of each other, they had always spent much time together, first as children, then when Periquine came home from school in the holidays and found that in the near vicinity there were few companions of his own age.

He had treated Fenella as if she were a small boy, compelling her to do his bidding, fag for him, run after him, fetch and carry, and because there was no-one else to be his confidante.

Now without really thinking about it they were back on the old easy terms they had always known.

"How much money have you got, Periquine?" Fenella asked.

"None, absolutely none!" he declared. "After I had seen Swayer, I gave up the rooms I had taken in Dover Street, sacked my valet, sold all my horses except the two I have driven down here today and paid up the greater part of my debts."

He paused a moment. Then he said, almost speaking to himself:

"I curse myself for being such a fool as to give that 'bit o' muslin' two gowns she fancied only two weeks ago. But how could I know that things were so desperate?"

"You still have the Priory," Fenella said hesitantly.

"Yes, I still have the Priory," Lord Corbury answered. "But I could not sell it even if I wished to because it is entailed to my son. The son I am not likely ever to be able to afford!"

"At least it is a roof over your head."

"And I should be grateful for that," Lord Corbury agreed ironically. "I also have a thousand unproductive acres of land which I cannot afford to farm myself and certainly am unlikely to find tenants who will do it for me. Do you realise, Fenella, that since the war all over the country farmers are going bankrupt?"

"I do realise it," Fenella answered, "and I think it is disgraceful! While we were at war with the

French we all needed food and were grateful if the farmers could feed the country. Yet now in 1817 only two years after Waterloo, the same men who were cheered and acclaimed cannot even raise a loan to carry them over the harvest."

"They say the country banks are going broke one after another," Lord Corbury said, "so you can hardly expect them to grant loans which are never likely to be repaid."

Fenella sighed.

"What are you going to do?"

"That is what I am asking you," he answered.

"I was hoping that when you came home you would be able to help people on your estate. But it does not now appear you will be able to do so."

"What people?" Lord Corbury asked without much interest in his voice.

"Well, the most important is Mrs. Buckle," Fenella answered. "After all, Periquine, she is your responsibility. She has been at the Priory for nearly fifty years. She first came when she was twelve as a scullery-maid to your grandfather."

"What is the matter with her?" Lord Corbury asked. "I saw her when I arrived and she seems all right to me."

"She is all right in her health," Fenella answered. "It is Simon, her son. You know how she dotes on him."

"I understood he came through the war without a scratch."

"He did and he married a girl from the next village last year. As he wanted to earn a living, he borrowed twenty pounds so that he could buy a horse and cart and set up as the local carrier. The old man who used to be the carrier died two years ago."

"Well, what is wrong with that?" Lord Corbury enquired.

"There is nothing wrong with it except that he went to Isaac Goldstein, who is one of your new tenants. He rented the Old Mill House."

"The Old Mill," Lord Corbury said wrinkling his forehead. "I thought that was too dilapidated for anyone to take."

"He pays only a very small rent for it," Fenella said, "and he is the horridest man you can possibly imagine. I would never have let him put a foot on the estate, if it had been anything to do with me. But Johnson let him the house because, I imagine, he was desperate for tenants. Periquine, he is a Usurer!"

"Here in Little Coombe!" Lord Corbury exclaimed. "Good heavens, what do we want a Usurer for?"

"We do not," Fenella answered, "except for someone like Simon. Mr. Goldstein goes regularly to Brighton and all the towns nearby, and I understand he has a thriving business. But he is crooked, really crooked, and that is what is so wrong."

Lord Corbury moved a little way from the window obviously interested in what she was saying.

"What do you mean he is crooked?"

"Well Simon borrowed twenty pounds from him a year ago," Fenella answered, "and Mr. Goldstein says he now owes him a hundred, and it goes up every month."

She made a gesture with her hands.

"How can Simon possibly pay him back £100? An you do see that however hard he works he gets deeper and deeper into debt."

"It is their usual method of extortion," Lord Corbury exclaimed, "I may be a fool in many ways, Fenella, but I have never been so cork-brained as to get into the clutches of Usurers. I have seen only too often what they have done to my brother-officers. One chap actually committed suicide because they squeezed him dry and went on threatening until he just could not pay any more."

Fenella clasped her hands together.

"I knew you would understand, Periquine," she said, "and that is why I hoped you would do something when you came home."

"What can I do," Lord Corbury asked. "I certainly cannot give Simon £100!"

"It is worse than that, it is not only Simon," Fenella said.

"Who else is involved?" Lord Corbury enquired.

"Well, you remember Mrs. Jarvis who kept the 'Green Man'?"

"I remember Jarvis well," Lord Corbury replied.

"He died about five years ago, but Mrs. Jarvis carried on by herself. She had Joe, her son, to help her until he went to the war. But she managed after he left and she saved every penny she made for him, so that when he came home he could take his father's place."

"What happened?" Lord Corbury asked.

"Mrs. Jarvis fell ill in the winter before last. It was very cold, and I think she economised on coal so as to save more money. Anyway she got pneumonia, and when she was dying Isaac Goldstein came to see her."

"Why should he do that?" Lord Corbury asked.

"It appeared he was married to her sister, and whether she sent for him or whether he just chanced to drop in I do not know. Anyway she gave him her money in safe keeping for Joe when he came back from the war. She also asked him to look after the Inn or, if it had to be sold, to keep the purchase money for Joe too."

"Go on," Lord Corbury said.

"Mrs. Jarvis died and when Joe came back and was told what his mother had arranged, Isaac Goldstein said that his mother had left him nothing."

"It is impossible!" Lord Corbury exclaimed. "How could he get away with it?"

"Apparently he just said to Joe, 'You prove that she gave me any money or that she wished you to have the proceeds of the sale of the "Green Man."'"

"He had sold it then."

"Yes he sold it a week after Mrs. Jarvis died, and according to local gossip he sold it well. But of course no-one knows for certain. It was quite a flourishing little Inn in its way, and there was also the money she had saved. Joe reckons it must have been over a thousand pounds in all and he has not had a penny."

"This is the most disgraceful thing I have ever heard!" Lord Corbury exclaimed, "I would like to tell this man Goldstein what I think of him."

"A lot of people have tried to do that," Fenella said, "but it does not do any good. He does not care, he is rich and he is a miser. I have seen him . . ."

She stopped suddenly and her face lit up.

"Listen! Periquine! I have an idea!"

"What is it?" he asked.

"I have thought of how you can get back the money for Simon Buckle, for Joe Jarvis, and perhaps make some for yourself."

"What are you talking about?" Lord Corbury enquired.

Fenella rose from the sofa to stand with her hands clasped together, her green eyes staring across the room as if she was concentrating fiercely.

"I know where Isaac Goldstein hides his money," she said. "I have seen him come back from his trips to the coast and take bags and bags from his cart, carry then into the house and hide them under the floor-boards."

"How on earth have you seen that?" Lord Corbury enquired.

Fenella drew a deep breath.

"I have told you he is a horrible man. Well, he has two very fierce dogs who guard his house when he is away, to protect his money of course. But, Periquine, he does not feed them properly. I suppose he thinks it keeps them savage if they are hungry. He gives them little enough when he is there, but when he is away they often go for three or four days without food and sometimes even water."

"The dirty swine! But what can you do about it?" Lord Corbury said.

"I feed them," Fenella answered.

"You feed them!" he repeated incredulously.

"I started by throwing them food over the fence," Fenella explained. "So now when they see me they wag their tails and I can do anything I like with them. Of course Isaac Goldstein does not know this."

"But you are quite certain they would not hurt you?" Lord Corbury asked.

"I really believe now they would protect me against anyone else," Fenella smiled. "But do you not see, Periquine, it makes it so easy! We will take Goldstein's ill-gotten money, give Jarvis and Simon what they are owed and perhaps there will be enough over for you to do at least a few repairs to the farms."

"Are you suggesting I should steal?" Lord Corbury asked in a voice of thunder.

"I am suggesting that you should take from the rich and give to the poor," Fenella retorted.

"I have never heard such a ridiculous idea in the whole of my life!" Lord Corbury exclaimed. "You do not suppose I would stoop to being a thief, do you?"

"Well, if you will not do so, Simon will remain in the clutches of this monster," Fenella said, "and Joe Jarvis is in such depths of despair that he just drinks away every penny he earns while he ruminates over the manner that he has been treated."

"I should have thought he could do something better than that," Lord Corbury remarked.

"What can he do?" Fenella enquired. "There was no witness present in the room when Mrs. Jarvis handed over the money, only we all know in the village how hard she worked, and how she saved every penny for her Joe. We also know that she certainly would not have wanted her brother-in-law, whom she hardly knew, to sell 'The Green Man' and put the money in his pocket."

"Perhaps I could speak to a lawyer on young Jarvis's behalf," Lord Corbury suggested.

"And how will you pay him?" Fenella enquired.

Lord Corbury made an impatient exclamation and walked towards the window.

"I must say, Periquine, I think you have grown very old," a soft voice said behind him.

"What do you mean by that?" he demanded.

"We used to do some daring things together," Fenella answered. "Do you remember when we stole all the prize peaches from the Lord Lieutenant's greenhouse because his gardener was so offensive to all the poorer people who entered for the Flower Show and made certain they never had a chance of winning anything? We ate some of the peaches and threw the rest in the lake. No-one ever discovered who the thieves were."

"We were young then," Lord Corbury said.

"And another time you took your father's horses without his knowledge and we drove to a Mill on the Downs. It was one of the most wonderful days I have ever spent in my whole life, Periquine. Do you remember how exciting it was?"

"It was indeed," he answered. "Thirty-eight rounds and both bruisers so exhausted at the end they could hardly strike at each other."

"We drove the horses home," Fenella said, "and because old Sam the groom was fond of us he never gave us away. I remember when your father asked what we had been doing, you said we had been fishing. At least you were not afraid in those days."

"Damn you, I am not afraid! But stealing is just not the sort of thing a gentleman does."

"It is not much use being a gentleman with only pride in your pocket," Fenella said.

"It is the only thing left for me," Lord Corbury said bitterly.

"Well, it will not get you very far with Hetty," Fenella said. "It is not only Sir Virgil who is ambitious."

Lord Corbury turned round angrily from the window.

"You will not say anything against Hetty. She is perfect! The most beautiful, the most wonderful, the most adorable creature on whom any man has ever set eyes. I have known a lot of women since I have been away, Fenella, but there has never been anyone as beautiful as Hetty."

"Yes she is very . . . beautiful," Fenella agreed with a little sigh on the words.

"You would not be bad-looking, Fenella, if you took a little more trouble with yourself," Lord Corbury said with the critical familiarity of a brother. "Why do you not get yourself a new gown and take more trouble over your hair."

"A new gown!" Fenella laughed. "You seem to have forgotten my condition is very much the same as yours."

"I am quite certain your father is not bankrupt," Lord Corbury retorted.

"Oh, he is not bankrupt," Fenella answered, "but he has no money to spend on frills and furbelows for his daughter. He is intent at the moment on buying a first edition of Milton's 'Paradise Lost'. Three months ago it was a first edition of Francis Bacon and the month before that a very expensive volume of Alexander Pope."

"But if you are eighteen, surely your mother wants you to meet people and go out into Society."

"Mama!"

Fenella threw up her hands.

"You have been away a long time, Periquine. You know Mama is only interested in her garden. She is buying some special lilies from China. The Azaleas which arrived last week from India cost an absolute fortune. Papa and Mama still behave as they did when I was a child—as if I did not exist. When they remember I am there, they send me on an errand."

"Poor Fenella, it was always the same, was it not?" Lord Corbury said.

He moved beside her, put his arm round her shoulder and gave her an affectionate hug.

"Well, we seem to be in the same plight!" he said. "Which, if you think about it, is nothing new."

"We used to manage to have some fun all the same," Fenella said softly.

"We will have some more in the future," Lord Corbury promised.

There was a silence while he was still holding Fenella close against him.

"Mrs. Buckle has not had any wages for nine months," Fenella said quietly, "and she told me to ask you for something with which to pay the tradespeople. Since the game-keepers all left, there have not been any rabbits or pigeons off the estate, although of course you can go out and shoot some."

"If I can afford the cartridges," Lord Corbury said bitterly.

He released Fenella and then stood staring down at her.

"How much risk is there in taking this money you were talking about?" he asked.

Fenella gave a little cry of delight.

"You will do it? Oh, Periquine, I knew you would! Even if there is not a penny over for yourself, you will be able to help Joe and Simon, and perhaps there will be enough to pay Mrs. Buckle and old Headstone, the butcher. He told me to tell you he would be deeply obliged for even a little towards his account."

"Curse you, it is crazy!" Lord Corbury said. "But it does not appear as if I have much alternative. Is there anything in the house left to sell, Fenella?"

"Not unless you sell the beds," she said, "and they will not fetch much. The hangings are all moth-eaten and every blanket is full of holes, as I found when I helped Mrs. Buckle make your bed."

"You knew I was coming?" Lord Corbury asked sharply.

"I knew you would come soon after Mr. Swayer had seen you. He came down last week and had a look round."

Lord Corbury was silent for a moment, and then he said:

"Well if I have to be hanged, I may as well make it worth their while. When do we start on this crazy robbery of yours?"

"Isaac Goldstein went away to-day," Fenella answered. "That means that he is very unlikely to return before the day after tomorrow. It would be safest if we went tomorrow."

"You had it all planned out for me, did you not?" Lord Corbury said accusingly.

"No, I swear to you I only thought of it at this moment," Fenella answered. "And you know quite well I did not expect you home quite so soon, or I should not have had to hide in the Priest's Hole when Hetty arrived."

Lord Corbury looked at her searchingly to see if she was telling the truth.

"If I thought this was one of your plots to get me into trouble, Fenella—" he began.

"No, Periquine, no!" she interrupted. "You know I do not wish you to get into trouble. That anyway is a most unfair thing to say, because in the past half the time I took the blame for your misdeeds. What about when your cricket-ball went through the Church window? You would not own up because you said your father would have you flogged at Eton for it."

"Good Lord, what a memory you have!" Lord Corbury said. "That was years ago."

"I have not forgotten anything," Fenella said, "and I have been hoping that when you came back it would be just like old times."

"At least in those days I had a father who paid for things," Lord Corbury said. "Now I have to find the money myself."

"And you will find it . . . I know you will!" Fenella cried enthusiastically. "You have always been clever. Periquine, you always had a quick brain. Look how well you did at school! And the Duke of Wellington said you were one of the best Captains he ever had under his command."

"Fat lot of use it is now!" Lord Corbury said disagreeably.

"I think you are being unduly despondent," Fenella said. "You will think of something brilliant sooner or later. Meanwhile let us collect a little money. You could call it a . . . fund for . . . Hetty if you . . . like."

She spoke the last words hesitatingly and she saw Lord Corbury's eyes light up.

"That is a good idea, Fenella," he said. "I will collect money somehow, even by the most nefarious means, and when I have enough I can go to Sir Virgil and ask him for Hetty's hand. It will not seem so reprehensible if I am doing it so that I can marry her."

"No of course it will not," Fenella agreed, "and you do . . . love her . . . very, very much . . . do you not?"

"You know I do," Lord Corbury said. "And if it means I can marry her, I swear to you, Fenella, I shall not quibble at robbing the Bank of England!"

"Then you must indeed . . . love her," Fenella said in a very small voice.

Chapter Two

Lord Corbury, sitting in front of the fire with a glass of wine in his hand, heard a noise at the window. He turned his head to see Fenella clambering through the casement.

"Why do you not come in at the door?" he enquired, only to perceive the answer to his question as she came towards him.

She was wearing pantaloons and a tightly buttoned jacket. With her slim figure she looked very much like a small boy.

"Good heavens!" Lord Corbury ejaculated.

"They are yours," Fenella explained. "You wore them last when you were at Eton."

She laughed and added:

"Do not look so shocked! You must realise that long skirts are not conducive to climbing through the fan-light of the door, which is what I shall have to do."

"Well I only hope no-one sees you," Lord Corbury said.

He made no effort to rise but lay back in his chair, and Fenella knew by the expression on his face that he was feeling depressed.

"What has happened?" she asked as she reached his side. "Did Hetty not come this afternoon?"

"She came," Lord Corbury replied.

"And she has upset you?"

"She made me feel how impossible it is for me

ever to contemplate marrying her," Lord Corbury said sourly.

"What did she say?" Fenella enquired.

"She did not put it into so many words," Lord Corbury replied, "but I received the impression that no suitor with less than £50,000 in the bank would be acceptable to her father."

Fenella pursed her lips together to prevent herself from saying aloud what she thought. After a moment Lord Corbury went on:

"I may as well acknowledge defeat right away! What is the point of fighting when there is not a chance of winning?"

"That is exactly what we might have said in England during the war," Fenella answered. "Who would have thought that a little island like ours, so tiny on the map, could defeat the might of Bonaparte when he had already conquered nearly the whole of Europe."

There was a pause. Then Lord Corbury said:

"You are very sweet, Fenella, and somehow you always manage to cheer me up. Do you really believe in miracles?"

"Of course I do," Fenella declared, "especially where you are concerned. I am sure, Periquine, that God helps those who help themselves."

"So you are still intent on this madcap robbery?" Lord Corbury said.

"Do you suppose I have dressed myself up like this just to sit beside you in heavy gloom?" Fenella enquired.

She looked at Lord Corbury's glass and added suspiciously:

"You are not drinking to drown your sorrows, are you?"

"Precious little chance of that," Lord Corbury replied. "This is the last bottle in the cellar. After tonight I shall not be able to drink anything but water."

"After tonight things may be very different," Fenella said.

She walked across the room to the window.

"We must start soon. We ought to arrive at the old Mill when it is dusk but not too dark for us to see out way to the house. We also have to go through the wood."

Lord Corbury tossed back the rest of the wine that was in his glass.

"Let us get going," he said recklessly. "Do you want me to wear some sort of fancy-dress?"

Fenella regarded him critically. He might be poor but at the moment he appeared as elegant and as exquisitely garbed as any Beau she had ever seen.

Then she remembered that when these clothes were worn out he would not be able to afford others.

"Put on the oldest things you have, Periquine," she said. "We have got to climb over a fence and I will have to stand on your shoulders to get in through the fan-light. You will find some of the garments you wore before you went into the Army upstairs in your closet. I tidied them only last week. And wear a black cravat—it is far less noticeable than what you have on now."

"I suppose there is sense in what you are saying," Lord Corbury said grudgingly.

He went from the room and Fenella heard him going upstairs.

She picked up his empty glass and carried it to a tray which stood on a side-table. Then she looked round the room to see if there was anything else she could tidy.

She had been over during the morning and had made the Saloon appear as habitable as possible. There were bowls of flowers on the table, and while the cushions were old and worn they were clean because she had washed and pressed them herself.

Yet there was no doubt the whole place looked sadly shabby, and she knew only too well how it must appear in Hetty's eyes.

The Priory was, Fenella thought, as far as she was concerned, the most beautiful place in the world. After the Dissolution of the monasteries in the reign of Henry VIII, the King had given the Priory and its estates to one of his courtiers who had served him well, and invested him with a Knighthood.

By a miracle the Priory and its lands had remained in the hands of the family through the troublesome times of Cromwell's dictatorship, and on his Restoration Charles II created the barony of Corbury.

"However poor Periquine may be," Fenella told herself, "I am glad that he cannot sell the Priory or dispose of its lands."

Somehow she felt sure that something would happen which would enable him one day to live in his home in the style in which he wished to do. She could only pray that that day was not too far ahead.

She knew Periquine so well. She knew how easily he got depressed, how quickly his spirits would rise again. But there was a depth, although he was not really aware of it, in his character and a resilience which would eventually, she was certain, carry him through to victory.

"He must succeed, he must!" she told herself, and then with a drop of her heart realised that success for Periquine meant that he would marry Hetty.

It was hard to contemplate Periquine being married to anyone, but least of all to the girl they had both known since they were children.

Hetty Baldwyn had always been spoilt and had shown it by her air of disdain and condescension towards other girls, and the manner in which she assumed as her right that every man of her acquaintance should be at her feet.

While Periquine had been away with the Army in France, Hetty had captivated all the young men of the neighbourhood and had then gone to London to captivate the *Beau Monde*.

"It is understandable that Periquine cannot resist her," Fenella told herself now.

She thought of Hetty's classical features, golden hair, unblemished skin, and knew she was not likely to be missed by Periquine's roving eye once he returned from the war.

"All I want is his happiness," Fenella thought,

but she knew if she was honest with herself that she did not feel he would find happiness with Hetty Baldwyn.

She was still standing in the Saloon with a worried expression in her green eyes when Lord Corbury came downstairs again.

He had obeyed her instructions and was wearing a very old pair of pantaloons which Fenella knew had been darned on one leg.

He had on a jacket which having been made for him some years ago, was slightly too small. A black cravat encircled his throat and was tied in an elegant knot on the front of his shirt.

Nevertheless he managed to look smart because he wore his clothes with an air and they seemed to accentuate the raffish glint which was never far from his eye.

Fenella gave a little laugh.

"Can this really be the Robber Chief in person?" she asked mockingly.

"If you say any more," Lord Corbury replied, "I will give you what I used to give my fag at Eton who looked just like you in that suit—six of the best."

"I am sure you were a bully," Fenella retorted, "and if you stay here bullying me we shall never reach the Old Mill before it is too dark for the dogs to differentiate between friend and foe."

"Oh Lord, the dogs!" Lord Corbury ejaculated. "I had forgotten them!"

"I had not," Fenella answered. "I have brought them some food, it is outside the window."

"Do we have to enter and leave the house in this surreptitious manner?" Lord Corbury enquired.

"You can go out through the door if you like," Fenella answered, "but I certainly do not want Mrs. Buckle or old Barnes to see me. Not that I expect that they would move from the kitchen fire at that very moment."

"Let us take no chances," Lord Corbury said with an air of resignation.

He followed Fenella over the window-sill and out onto the terrace outside.

Being so small she had some difficulty in clambering out while he could almost do it in one stride.

There was a basket on the moss-covered flagstones and Fenella picked it up.

"I hope you have brought plenty," Lord Corbury said.

"There are always masses of scraps at home," Fenella answered, "our cook is very extravagant."

"It is more than Mrs. Buckle is ever likely to be," Lord Corbury said bitterly. "As she informed me tonight she cannot cook what she had not got."

"Poor Periquine, are you hungry?" Fenella asked.

"Not at the moment," Lord Corbury replied, "but I have a suspicion that by the end of the week I shall be setting rabbit-snares with old bits of wire, and trying to charm pigeons down from the nest."

"No cartridges!" Fenella said perceptively.

"Only a few," Lord Corbury answered. "God knows I have never seen a house containing so little of everything."

There was a bitterness in his tone which told Fenella that he must have made an inspection of the place during the day and she wondered if it was after Hetty had left in the afternoon.

Perhaps she had not stayed for long. Lord Corbury had been cheerful enough when she had left him to go home for luncheon.

"I have not told Papa and Mama you are here yet," she had said. "Not that they would be particularly interested, but I thought the fewer people who knew, the less likely there would be of Sir Virgil hearing of your arrival."

"That was thoughtful of you," Lord Corbury approved. "The only thing I have to live for is Hetty's visits and if she does not come to see me I shall feel like blowing a hole through my head."

Fenella did not answer this. She had only hoped that Hetty would make an effort to go to the Priory during the afternoon.

She would not do so, Fenella knew only too well, unless it suited her. If she herself wanted to see Periquine, she would get there whoever tried to stop her. It was a question of going out of her way to bring him any comfort. Fenella very much doubted if she would make an effort.

"I am being catty," she told herself. "I must not be unkind about Hetty. And I must not be jealous of her because she is so beautiful."

Even as she thought of it, Fenella knew it was not Hetty's beauty that made her jealous, but the fact that Periquine was interested in her.

Always in the past when he had been home he had seemed to belong to her, there being few distractions to take him from her side.

She had gone out shooting with him in the Autumn, she had sat beside him when he fished in the summer. They had rowed a boat on the lake and ridden their horses through the woods.

Merely country interests, country pursuits! And yet Fenella could never remember a time when either of them seemed bored. There had always been something interesting to do.

But now Periquine was depressed. That she could understand, where money was concerned. But it was not like him to have lost his enthusiasms, and not to be amused by ordinary everyday things which had entertained him in the past.

They walked across the lawn side by side in silence. The sun was sinking behind a great wood of fir trees in a blaze of crimson, gold and saffron.

Already the sky overhead was a translucent blue and the first evening star twinkled faintly in the midst of it.

"There is nothing more lovely," Fenella thought, "than the Priory in May."

There was the fragrance of lilacs, the heavy scent of syringa, and everywhere that she looked there were patches of colour in shrubs and trees which while undoubtedly overgrown, were nevertheless very lovely.

As they walked along moving towards Robins

Wood that lay parallel to the long drive which ran to the Highway, she thought that the peace and beauty of the evening was having a soothing effect on her companion.

After they crossed a narrow bridge over a stream which fed the lake she said:

"There are some very fat trout since you last fished here."

"Are there?"

She thought that Lord Corbury's eyes lit up.

"Then I must certainly have a try at them. It is so long since I had a rod in my hand that I dare say I have lost the art of hooking a fish."

"I expect it will come back to you," Fenella said.

He looked at her and smiled.

"Forgive me for being so blue-devilled," he said beguilingly, "I realise you are trying to cheer me up, and even if you cannot do so, I have no right to inflict my miseries on you."

"It is not a question of inflicting anything on me," Fenella answered. "We have always shared our difficulties in the past."

She looked up at him as if she hoped he would agree with her, but now he was watching the rooks coming in to roost and merely said absently:

"Yes, of course."

They moved into Robin's Wood, which was now thickly overgrown as the trees should have been thinned years before.

There was a twisting path between the tree-trunks and they followed it. It grew darker and still darker as the sun dipped into the horizon, and the evening light did not percolate through the thick branches above them.

It was as they were moving without speaking that they heard someone coming. Fenella stood still, and quickly Lord Corbury, with a reaction which must have come from his service training, took her arm and pulled her behind a thick briar-bush.

"Who can it be?" he whispered.

"I have no idea," Fenella answered. "There is never anyone in the woods at night."

The sound of someone moving rather slowly but heavily came nearer. Then they heard the murmur of a voice.

It seemed to Lord Corbury the words were foreign and then when the speaker was nearly level with them, he realized the man whoever he might be, was saying a prayer.

Restraining an impulse to raise his head to look, Lord Corbury still holding on to Fenella's arm remained crouched down beside her until the footsteps and the voice receded into the distance.

"It is quite all right," Fenella said, "it is only the old Vicar."

"The old Vicar?" Lord Corbury questioned.

"You must remember him. He was the Vicar of Little Coombe for years. Then he got so vague and absent-minded that the Bishop gave him charge of the Church-in-the-Wood."

"Do you mean the Monk's Chapel?" Lord Corbury asked.

"Of course. It is just as it used to be when we were children. It is still full of squirrels, birds and even rabbits. I often go there on a Sunday when the old Vicar, if he remembers, holds a service."

"Does anyone else go?" Lord Corbury enquired.

"There are two old women from the village who adore him, one of whom cleans his tiny house. It is little more than a hut, but he is happy there. The Parish had grown too much for him. He always forgot funerals, and someone invariably had to fetch him to a wedding long after the bride had arrived."

Lord Corbury laughed.

"That must have caused a great deal of trouble."

"It did," Fenella replied, "especially as the old Vicar was usually lost in the woods. You remember how he loved the animals? He still tames the squirrels, and the deer eat out of his hands."

"I must go and see him one day," Lord Corbury said. "I might have spoken to him just now."

"I thought of that but it is wisest that no-one sees us," Fenella said. "Isaac Goldstein is so crooked that I do not think he would dare make a fuss about his monies being stolen, but one never knows and it is safer if we are not seen anywhere in the vicinity."

"Quite right," Lord Corbury approved.

They went back onto the path and now it was getting very difficult to find their way.

Fenella went ahead and finally as they emerged through the trees, Lord Corbury saw ahead of them a high fence of over-lapping wattles.

"That was never there in the past," he ejaculated.

"No, Isaac Goldstein put it up," Fenella answered. "He said it was to keep the dogs in, but I have a suspicion it was to keep intruders out."

The Mill House looked very dilapidated. The stream ran by it on one side, on the other it was only a short distance from the Highway on a drive which had not been repaired for years.

Some of the windows had been boarded up, the others were dark and there was no sign of any light.

Fenella had the idea that Lord Corbury was feeling apprehensive.

"It is quite all right," she said soothingly. "I saw with my own eyes Mr. Goldstein go away and if he has been extorting money from his victims all day it is not likely he will drive home in the dark."

Lord Corbury had no answer to this logic and followed Fenella in silence to the fence. There he saw in one place a number of logs which had been placed against it and he guessed this was where Fenella climbed over when she was alone.

She handed him the basket and, as he expected, stepped up the logs and putting her hands on the top of the fence, threw her leg over.

Instantly there was a sudden snarling and barking below which sounded so ferocious that instinctively Lord Corbury put out his hands to prevent her going any further.

Fenella gave a little whistle.

"It is all right, boys," she said, "it is me."

At the sound of her voice, the snarling and barking ceased, and instead Lord Corbury could hear the
dogs jumping about making noises of welcome. When
he looked over the top he could see they were wagging
their tails.

In the dusk they certainly looked frightening.
One was a large wolfhound, the other a huge mongrel
of doubtful extraction. Both had large jaws and sharp
teeth and Lord Corbury had little doubt they would
dispose very effectively of any intruder they did not
welcome.

"The basket!" Fenella said as she jumped down
to the ground. Lord Corbury handed it to her, while
the dogs slobbering with excitement danced around
her.

She gave them some food which they gobbled up
with such speed that it was obvious they were both
extremely hungry.

"Come over," she said, "I will not let them hurt
you."

"I hope you are sure of that," Lord Corbury replied a little dryly. "I have a great objection to form-
ing part of a dog's dinner."

"There is plenty for them here," Fenella said, "and
I will protect you."

Lord Corbury put his leg over the fence and
waited. One of the dogs looked towards him and gave
a little growl in his throat.

"It is a friend," Fenella admonished him, patting
his head as she spoke.

She gave him another large piece of meat and
an equal portion to the other dog.

"All right!" she said.

Lord Corbury rather apprehensively lowered himself down to the ground.

"Keep near to me," Fenella commanded. "They
have accepted you or they would have sprung at you
by now."

"That is undoubtedly re-assuring," Lord Corbury
remarked.

He stood close to Fenella while she finally took

two large bones from her basket and handed one to
each dog.

"That will keep them busy," she smiled.

She threw the empty basket back over the
fence and led the way towards the house.

It was certainly in a bad state, Lord Corbury
noticed. The wood was crumbling away from the windows and the garden that had been there in the Mill-
Keeper's time was non-existent. A chimney-pot had
been blown down and lay smashed on the path that
led to the front door.

"I cannot believe that Mr. Goldstein is a particularly good tenant," he said.

"He is a miser," Fenella answered.

When they reached the front door, Fenella
looked up and Lord Corbury followed her glance.

There was a fan-light over the top of the door
which had rusted away and which he could see was
broken at the sides. The glass from it had gone and it
was stuffed with old rags.

The aperture however looked very narrow and
he wondered if anyone, even as slim as Fenella, could
squeeze through it.

As if she read his thoughts she said:

"I am sure I can do it. Let me get on your shoulders."

Lord Corbury bowed his back and she climbed
up on him as she had done so often when she had
been a child, and as he straightened himself holding
on to her ankle he realised that she was very little
heavier then she had been last time he had supported
her.

On that occasion they had been climbing over
the wall at the Lord Lieutenant's garden to steal his
peaches. Lord Corbury could only hope that this
raid was to be equally successful.

Fenella had pushed the fan-light to one side.
Now she started to squeeze herself through it while
Lord Corbury watched her anxiously.

As her legs in her tight pantaloons disappeared
inside, he wondered what would hapen if they were

discovered, but after that he had no time for being introspective.

He heard Fenella reach the floor with a little thud.

"I shall not be able to open the door," she called. "I will open one of the windows."

A moment later Lord Corbury saw her at a casement and she pushed it out with some difficulty.

He helped her pull it wide, then stepped into the room.

"I have brought a candle," Fenella said feeling inside the pocket of her jacket. "Pull the curtains."

The curtains were heavy and dark. Having lit one candle Fenella found two others and lit those too.

It was an extraordinary room. As Lord Corbury looked round it he realised it must be furnished with things which Isaac Goldstein had extorted from his creditors when they could not afford to pay him in cash.

There were arm-chairs covered in expensive brocades, none of which matched. There was an inlaid table which was undoubtedly valuable on which all sorts of strange objects were crowded together.

There was a small marble statue, a bronze dog, a beautiful piece of Dresden china, a Chelsea angel with its head broken and quite a number of snuff boxes on some of which the initials of their previous owners were encircled in diamonds.

"Good Heavens—Aladdin's Cave!" Lord Corbury ejaculated.

He saw a pile of pictures standing against the wall, and in another corner a suit of armour beside a stuffed bear.

"We cannot take any of those," Fenella said in a practical tone. "They could be easily traced if we tried to sell them."

She was down on her knees as she spoke pulling back the hearth-rug. Then her small hands were trying to lift one of the floor boards.

"Let me do that," Lord Corbury said.

He raised the board, then gave a whistle.

In the flickering light of the candles it was easy to see there were a large number of canvas bags piled into a small aperture.

"I brought a pillow-case with me," Fenella said, pulling it out from the inside pocket of her black jacket.

"You are obviously very experienced," Lord Corbury remarked. "Do we take all these bags?"

"As many as we can carry," Fenella replied. "It is no use stopping to investigate but they may only contain silver, in which case we shall want a large number to find a thousand pounds for Joe Jarvis."

"You are right," Lord Corbury agreed. "What is more, let us be quick about it and get out of here."

The pillow-case was made of strong linen but even so when it was nearly full with the canvas bags, Fenella looked at it a little anxiously.

"I hope it will not burst."

"So do I," Lord Corbury agreed. "It is monstrously heavy."

He put back the floor board and Fenella adjusted the hearth-rug. Lord Corbury carried the pillow-case to the window, pulled back the curtains and leaning over the sill set it down on the ground outside.

He found himself being watched benignly by the two dogs wagging their tails.

"Your friends seem to approve of our action," he said, "whatever their owner may say."

"Let us hurry," Fenella pleaded, "but first I must put back the fan-light."

There was a tremor of fear in her voice which Lord Corbury did not miss.

"I will do it," he said.

He took a chair from the room, and carrying it into the narrow hall he climbed on it and pushed the fan-light back into place. He then stuffed the rags into the holes where they had been before.

When he came back Fenella was already outside patting the dogs.

He blew out the candles, climbed out after her and pulled the window to.

"Will Goldstein notice it is not clasped?" he asked.

"When he gets as far as discovering that it will not matter," Fenella replied.

Lord Corbury bent and picked up the pillow-case. It was, as he had already said, extremely heavy, so heavy it was almost impossible for him to walk upright as they progressed towards the fence.

They had almost reached it when they heard in the distance the sound of wheels. For a moment Fenella thought she must be mistaken. But then there was no doubt. There was not only the noise of wheels but echo of horses hooves. They were coming down the rough drive from the road towards the house!

"Quickly," she began to say to Lord Corbury, then realised that his hearing and instinct was as quick if not quicker than hers.

Already he had thrown the pillow-case over the fence and now without even speaking he picked her up in his arms and deposited her on top of it.

Then as she slithered down on the other side he followed her.

They had only just put the fence between themselves and the Mill House when they heard the cart and horse come to a standstill.

At the same time the dogs barking at the tops of their voices ran towards it. If she had been doubtful before as to who was arriving, Fenella knew as she heard the sound the dogs were making that it was Isaac Goldstein.

It was true they were barking, but they were barking with the welcoming sound a dog makes when someone comes home, not the ferocious menacing tones with which they greet an intruder.

In the darkness she put out her hands to touch Lord Corbury.

"I thought you said he never came home at night," he said with a mocking note in his voice.

"I am . . . sorry, Periquine," she murmured humbly.

"No need to be sorry," he said. "We are safe at any rate for the moment! I do not think I have ever been quite so near to having a rope round my neck."

Fenella shuddered. For the first time the adventure seemed foolhardy and yet they so far had succeeded.

She knew that Lord Corbury was searching on the ground for any bags which might have fallen from the pillow-case when he had thrown it over the fence.

He found them and slung the heavy burden once again over his shoulder.

"Come on," he said in a low voice, "the sooner we get away from the scene of the crime the better."

It was not very easy to find their way back through the wood. Fenella walked ahead and after a little while Lord Corbury put his free hand on her shoulder.

"I used to rather fancy my night eyes in the war," he said, "but here I feel as blind as a bat."

"I know the way," Fenella answered confidently.

Nevertheless there were moments when she put out her hands as if to make quite sure they were on the path and not walking directly into the trunk of a tree.

Finally they emerged onto the side of the stream, crossed the bridge and went back through the gardens toward the Priory.

The stars were coming out, and as they moved across what had once been a smooth lawn Fenella could smell the scent of stocks. She threw back her head to look up at the sky and said a little prayer of thankfulness.

It might have been wrong to commit a robbery, but she was sure that in this case the end justified the means.

The casement-window of the Saloon was still open, the candles were still glowing golden against the mellow wood of the old panelling. It looked very cosy and secure.

Lord Corbury dumped the pillow-case down on the hearth-rug and threw a log onto the smouldering ashes.

Fenella sat down on the floor and the flames, startled into life, shimmered on the curls of her red hair.

For a moment there was silence. Then she looked up at Lord Corbury, her eyes sparkling with excitement, her lips smiling.

"We have done it! Oh, Periquine, we have done it!"

"By the skin of our teeth," he said soberly. "Do you realise, Fenella, if they do not hang you for your part in what we have just done, you will certainly be transported."

"Stop moaning and let us see what we have brought back with us," Fenella said.

"You are a hopeless case of lawlessness!" he replied.

As his hands went out towards the pillow-case, Fenella jumped to her feet.

"Wait a moment!" she warned him.

She crossed the room to pull the curtains.

"I am not taking any chances," she explained. "That was how I saw where Isaac Goldstein hid his money. I was in the garden feeding the dogs when he came home unexpectedly. It was late afternoon, not yet dark, and he would have seen me if I had climbed over the fence. So I hid behind an elder-bush.

"I saw him carry these little bags into the house from his cart and because I was so curious I crept a little nearer to see what he was doing with them."

"Taking a quite unwarrantable risk," Lord Corbury observed with pretended severity.

"A risk which has turned to our advantage," Fenella replied.

"Open the bags, Periquine, I cannot wait to see if we have a thousand pounds for poor Joe."

Lord Corbury opened a bag. He looked inside,

then emptied the coins onto the hearth-rug between them. They were of gold!

"Start putting them into stacks of ten," he suggested. "It will be easier to count at the end."

Fenella did as she was told and Lord Corbury kept emptying the bags.

Four which he had noticed when he had lifted them from under the floor-board were lighter than the others, contained mostly bank-notes. Notes between one to five pounds in denomination. There was no silver, no copper coins, they were all gold.

By the time they reached the last canvas bag, both Lord Corbury and Fenella were working in silence. Then as she got to the last of her little stacks of ten golden sovereigns, Lord Corbury sorted out the notes.

"In this bag they are all fivers," he began. Then he gave a cry. "Good God!"

"What is it," Fenella asked.

"These are not worth five pounds as I first thought," Lord Corbury replied, "but fifty pounds each!"

"It cannot be true!" Fenella said.

"It is," he answered. "Our friend Goldstein must have some very large borrowers amongst his clientele."

"Count them, count them all quickly!" Fenella cried in an excited voice. ". . . And the sovereigns!"

Lord Corbury began to count. Finally in a tone of astonishment he said:

"I might be mistaken, Fenella, but I think there is over six thousand pounds."

"Periquine! Is that . . . true?"

"I will count again."

"But it is wonderful, too wonderful for words!" Fenella exclaimed. "It is everything we wanted and more."

There was silence. Then Lord Corbury said heavily:

"I cannot keep all this money."

Fenella sat back on her heels and looked at him across the hearth-rug.

"It is one thing to take a small sum from a man," he went on, "but this is almost a fortune."

There was silence for a moment and then Fenella said:

"I think there are two things you have forgotten."

"What are they?" Lord Corbury enquired.

"First that Isaac Goldstein has extorted this money from people who I am quite certain could not afford it, who got into his clutches and could not escape from him and whom he has treated like Joe Jarvis. And secondly we cannot possibly put it back!"

"No that is true," Lord Corbury agreed. "But I feel a cad."

She rose to her feet and looked up at him.

"Is that not slightly better than feeling a bankrupt?" she asked.

His eyes were serious as they met hers and then he began to laugh.

"Fenella, you are incorrigible! It was just the same when we were children. You always pushed me into danger and yet somehow you got me out of it."

He laughed as he spoke. Then he put his arms round Fenella and hugged her.

"You are an Imp of mischief," he said, "but, oh God, I am grateful for you!"

"It was fun! Say it was fun now the danger is over!" Fenella insisted.

He squeezed her even tighter, then released her and said:

"All right, it was fun, and now what do we do with our ill-gotten money."

"I have thought of everything," Fenella said in a breathless voice. "I shall tell Mrs. Buckle—which means she will tell the whole village, that just before you left London you won some money gaming. I am quite certain Swayer will have informed everyone that you have not a penny, so it is quite obvious that you will have to have a windfall from somewhere."

"That sounds sense!" Lord Corbury agreed. "Go on."

"Then you will send for Joe and tell him that as you have been lucky you want to refund his losses. And you will give Simon Buckle £100 to pay off Goldstein! At least he will get that amount back although he does not deserve it."

"I cannot help thinking your ideas on justice are slightly unbalanced," Lord Corbury replied, "but so far I am with you all the way. What do we do with the rest?"

There was silence for a moment and then Fenella said:

"You pay off all the tradesmen, you take out just enough to repair the farms so that you can let them —a few hundred will do that—and what is left is of course . . . the fund for . . . Hetty."

She spoke the last words in a low voice and did not look at Lord Corbury as she spoke.

"The Fund for Hetty," he replied softly, "and we might hide it in the Priests Hole. For the time being at any rate, it would not be wise to pay too much into the bank."

"It will be quite safe in the Priests Hole," Fenella said. "No-one knows of its existence beside you and me. Your father told no-one else and he only learnt it from his father."

"Then we are agreed," Lord Corbury said lightly.

He bent to pick up some of the sovereigns before he said:

"Unless of course you would like some of it. It is yours just as much as mine, Fenella, and I would like to buy you a present."

"No!" Fenella retorted sharply. "I would not touch a penny of it!"

She spoke so violently that he looked at her in astonishment, and seeing the surprise in his eyes she added:

"You have stolen it for . . . Hetty, we must never . . . forget . . . that."

Chapter Three

Fenella came downstairs with her work-basket in her hand and went into the Salon.

She had watched Hetty and Lord Corbury walk across the lawn and knew they were going where they had hidden themselves for the last two afternoons, in the arbour down by the lake where no-one would see them.

She had been upstairs tidying Lord Corbury's bedroom when she heard Hetty arriving.

She had gone to the top of the stairs and, being able to see without being seen, she had watched a Vision of loveliness step out of the chaise which was driven by a smartly liveried groom.

Hetty was wearing a diaphanous frock of pale blue which suited her fair beauty, and her bonnet was trimmed with tiny rose-buds which also graced the minute sunshade she held above her head.

The whole ensemble was extremely elegant and, as Fenella knew, fabulously expensive. But Sir Virgil was a rich man who grudged no expense which contributed to his daughter's famed beauty.

It was not surprising, Fenella thought with a little ache in her heart, that Lord Corbury hurrying from the Salon to greet his guest had stood staring down at her as if he was spellbound.

Hetty put a little basket she was carrying down on the table in the Hall.

"That is supposedly for Mrs. Buckle," she said. "Pour it away when I have left."

"You are lovely," Lord Corbury said with a sudden depth in his voice, "so lovely I cannot believe that you are true!"

Hetty gave him a provocative glance from under her eyelids.

"Suppose we go into the garden and . . . find out," she said very softly.

Fenella saw Lord Corbury reach out to take Hetty's hand in his and raise it to his lips. Then he drew her down the passage to the garden-door, and a few seconds later Fenella saw them walking across the uncut lawn.

They seemed out of place in the ill-kept garden, and yet the huge grey house with its ancient grey walls standing behind them, the wide sweep of the silver lake, the ancient oak trees in the park, were, Fenella thought, the perfect background for Periquine.

He was a part of it, a part from which he could never escape. He belonged to it so closely, so securely, that it was impossible to think of him without remembering that the Priory belonged to him and him to the Priory.

As the little sunshade and Periquine's high-crowned hat finally vanished from view, Fenella gave herself a shake and went back to the task of tidying up the mess that Periquine had left when he arose that morning.

He was finding it hard to manage without a valet.

He had always had a servant to look after him in the Army, and in the past there had always been valet and footmen to lay out his clothes, bring him crisply laundered neck-cloths, and polish his boots until he could see his face in them.

Now there was only old Barnes who was long past his work, and it was as much as he could do to attend to the Dining-room and to shuffle upstairs once a day with His Lordship's hot shaving-water.

Fenella looked round the big room which had belonged to Periquine's mother.

It was panelled, but Lord Corbury had painted the old oak white, and the big carved four-poster which had been there since the Restoration was a riot of gold cupids and entwined hearts.

The curtains were of blue velvet, faded and worn, but still the beauty of the colour warmed her heart.

The inlaid chest of drawers had been made in France two centuries earlier. Fenella always dusted it tenderly.

The place would have been chaos, she knew, if she had not come over every morning to tidy up, to see that the clothes Periquine had worn the day before were pressed, his boots cleaned, and to lay out his evening-clothes ready for him to change before dinner.

He did not realise that she did it for him, and did not question the fact that he was really put to very little discomfort by his newly straitened circumstances.

He was always glad to see her, and as if she had not already given herself enough to do, he invariably found her some further services. Today she had been late with her tasks because the morning had been so exciting.

They had deliberately waited two days to see if Isaac Goldstein made a fuss. They listened apprehensively expecting to hear rumours from the village that he had been robbed.

But when nothing was said, and when Fenella going down to the fence to feed the dogs had discovered he had gone away again, they decided it was safe to put their plans into operation.

Accordingly this morning Fenella had told Mrs. Buckle the glad news that Lord Corbury before he left London had won a large sum gaming and that the debt had been honoured within the usual week.

"That's real good news, Miss Fenella!" Mrs. Buckle exclaimed.

"Will you give me a list of everything that is owed to the tradesmen?" Fenella asked.

"That's not difficult, Miss," Mrs. Buckle replied. "I have it here in writing, set down and added up by Simon, because as you well knows I can't write. But it was not necessary, for it's written in me brain like words of fire, and I'm sure I could hardly sleep with a wondering how it can ever be paid."

"It is to be paid now," Fenella said with a smile.

When she had the list from Mrs. Buckle she had gone to Lord Corbury for the money.

He had taken the gold coins from the Priest's Hole. Without telling him Fenella had asked for more than they owed, because she knew that food must be bought at least for the week ahead, and she felt sure that Periquine would dislike having to keep continually breaking in to his "Fund for Hetty."

After that Lord Corbury had sent for Simon Buckle and given him £100 to pay back the loan he had obtained from Isaac Goldstein.

"Promise me one thing," Lord Corbury had said to the astonished young man.

"Anything Your Lordship wishes me to promise, M'Lord," Simon had replied, finding it hard to believe his good fortune.

"It is that you will never again get into the hands of the Usurers," Lord Corbury said. "Borrow from anyone rather than those sharks. They are extortioners who simply steal your money from you under the pretence of doing business."

"I'll not be such a knuckle-head another time, M'Lord," Simon said gruffly and found it almost impossible to express his gratitude.

If Simon Buckle was overwhelmed by Lord Corbury's generosity, it was nothing to the stupefaction of Joe Jarvis when he learnt His Lordship was to give him back what he thought he had lost for ever.

Fenella had insisted on being present at the interviews because it gave her such pleasure to realise that justice was being done.

She felt her eyes grow misty with tears when Joe Jarvis said with a rough sincerity:

"Oi'll never be able t'thank ye for this, M'Lord, but Oi'll serve ye for th' rest of me life!"

"Is there any chance of your getting back 'The Green Man'?" Lord Corbury enquired.

"Oi shouldn't be surprised M'Lord if Oi couldn't go in as a partner," Joe answered. "Th' man that bought it be a getting on in years, and Oi have heard he finds th' work too much for him."

"A partnership would be a good idea!" Lord Corbury remarked. "But, if he agrees to your suggestion, have a proper agreement with him, and before you sign anything bring it to me first."

"Oi'll do that, M'Lord. And thank ye, M'Lord, thank ye."

Joe hurried from the room as if he wished to be off to "The Green Man" to start negotiations, but Fenella knew it was because he was half afraid that he would disgrace himself by bursting into tears.

She looked at Lord Corbury as the door shut behind Joe.

"It was worth it," she said softly.

He smiled back at her.

"I am beginning to think so too," he answered, "although it makes me embarrassed when they thank me. After all it is not my money I am giving them."

"But you risked your neck to get it, and that after all is more valuable to you than anything else," Fenella said.

"That contention is of course unanswerable," Lord Corbury laughed.

The excitement of the morning was not yet over. Fenella had sent for Mr. Porritt the local builder, and he too was delighted when he heard that he was to repair the farms.

"I don't mind telling you, M'Lord," he said, "I and my two sons have been out of work these last three months. This job'll be a real blessing to us and I makes no bones about it!"

"Then do not over-charge me," Lord Corbury said, "and get it done as quickly as possible. I intend to advertise that the farms are to let."

"There's no need to do that, M'Lord," Mr. Porritt replied. "There be a young farmer over at Bugle End who has had his eye on the land that Mac-Donald farmed ever since he left. He even consulted me about doing the necessary repairs to the house and to the barn. But he had no cash laid by and I didn't dare give him credit, seeing as how farming be not doing well at the moment."

"Is he a good farmer?" Lord Corbury asked.

"He has that reputation and he be an honest man," Mr. Porritt replied. "I don't believe Your Lordship 'll be disappointed in him."

"Tell him to come and see me," Lord Corbury said.

"I wouldn't be surprised if there wasn't someone else from that part of the county who 'ld like Grimble's farm," Mr. Porritt went on. "Have I your Lordship's permission, M'Lord, to say you will consider any trustworthy applicant?"

"You have indeed," Lord Corbury answered, "and the sooner they are in, the better I shall be pleased. When the repairs on these farms are completed, Porritt, we will have to turn our attention to the others."

"There's a lot of work to be done, M'Lord," Mr. Porritt said shaking his head but obviously delighted at the idea.

"Let us start with the first two," Lord Corbury suggested, "then perhaps something can be done about the others."

Fenella looked at him a little apprehensively as the builder went from the room.

"The other farms are in a very bad way," she said.

"Damn it all, I have to have more money!" Lord Corbury ejaculated. "You know as well as I do, Fenella, the rents on this land have made a good income in the past and they should do so in the future."

"Yes, I know," Fenella agreed. "Have you any ideas?"

"I am thinking," he replied enigmatically.

Fenella did not press him.

'He would not be thinking of anything but Hetty now!' she told herself and she went into the Salon and sat down on the floor beside one of the windows.

She had noticed that the lining of one of the curtains was torn and showed beneath the damask.

The linings of all the curtains were in a disgraceful state, but even if they were replaced, Fenella knew it was hardly worth the expense since the curtains themselves had faded so that the edges were almost white.

The room had been very lovely when Periquine's mother was alive, but after six years' neglect there was so much to be done that Fenella's mind shied away from even contemplating what it would cost.

At least their mad adventure in stealing so much money from Isaac Goldstein had solved the immediate problem of Periquine having enough to eat, and there was after all always a roof over his head.

It was so wonderful to have him home again. Fenella could hardly bear to remember the nights during the War when she had laid awake wondering if he was in danger, thinking of him being wounded or even killed.

News had been very intermittent and it was a long time after the defeat of Napoleon in 1814, in which she knew his Regiment had taken part, before she heard he was safe and had come through the fighting without even a scratch.

That day she had gone to the little Church-in-the-Woods and thanked God with an almost passionate intensity that Periquine's life had been saved.

She had thought that he would come home when his father died, but the 9th Lord Corbury was laid in the family vault without his son being amongst the mourners.

Fenella had learnt with horror that the reason for Periquine's absence was that hostilities had been

resumed in France after Napoleon had landed in the
South.

Once again she was back on her knees praying
for his safety tossing and turning against her pillow
every night as she found it impossible to sleep.

Then at last came the victory of Waterloo and
the war was really over but still Periquine did not
return.

Now he was back and she tried not to feel too
glad that he could not marry Hetty as he wished to
do. If ever that happened she was well aware she
would be excluded from his life.

She wanted his happiness, she wanted it even
more than she wanted her own, and yet she knew to
live without being able to see and be with Periquine
would be like shutting out the sun.

She was so intent on her thoughts that she did
not hear the door open and jumped when a voice,
lofty and authoritative, said:

"I understand Miss Baldwyn is here."

Fenella looked up and saw standing in the
doorway a very impressive gentleman who she instantly concluded must be Sir Nicolas Waringham.

He was extremely smartly dressed and his hair was
arranged in the windswept manner adopted from
the Prince Regent. There was a stiff, somewhat pompous, dignity about him which made him easily rec-
ognisable from Lord Corbury's description.

Fenella realised as she stared that the newcomer was waiting for an answer to his question.

"Do you want to speak to Miss Baldwyn?" she
asked.

"I should have thought that was obvious unless
you are nit-witted," Sir Nicolas said sharply. "Hurry,
girl, and find her!"

His tone told Fenella all too clearly that he had
mistaken her for a servant, and without really thinking she replied mischievously in a broad Sussex accent:

"Aye, but us be real turnip-heads in th' countree."

Her impersonation was too broad to be anything

but ludicrous, and Sir Nicolas raised his quizzing-glass. Then he said in a different tone:

"I see I was mistaken. I must ask your pardon because I mistook you for a maid-servant."

Fenella rose to her feet.

"It was understandable," she said, "because I am busy with a humble task of sewing. At the same time may I introduce myself? I am Lord Corbury's cousin, Fenella Lambert."

"Then you are Lord Farquhar's niece!" Sir Nicolas exclaimed. "I know your uncle, Miss Lambert. He is most distinguished and a close friend of the Prince Regent."

Fenella had reached Sir Nicolas's side. She curtsied as she said:

"And you must be Sir Nicolas Waringham."

"You are correct in your assumption, Miss Lambert," Sir Nicolas replied. His bow was perfunctory and he barely bent his head.

Fenella was thinking quickly. It would certainly not do for Sir Nicolas to go in search of Hetty and Periquine.

He might surprise them in what would appear to him, since he was Hetty's suitor, to be a reprehensible situation. What was more, if he were to tell Sir Virgil there was no doubt that both Hetty and Periquine would be in trouble.

There was only one thing to do, Fenella decided: she must somehow keep Sir Nicolas engaged until they returned.

"I do not think Hetty will be long," she said evasively, "and I am so very interested to meet you."

"Indeed!" Sir Nicolas raised his quizzing-glass once again.

It was obvious he had not been impressed by Fenella's somewhat shabby appearance since she had been working upstairs in the bed-room, her hair was curling untidily round her forehead, and not at all in the decorous manner expected of a young lady of Fashion.

"Periquine has told me you have a most interesting ancestry," Fenella said.

For a moment she thought the hard and indifferent expression on Sir Nicolas's face relaxed a little.

"My family tree is in fact unique," he replied. "I am as I expect you know, the Premier Baronet of Great Britain. My ancestors were land-owners and Sheriffs before William the Conqueror invaded these shores."

"How thrilling," Fenella said, "it must make you very proud."

"Why not?" Sir Nicolas enquired.

He looked round the room as he spoke. His eyes seemed to miss nothing and Fenella thought there was a little curl of contempt on his lips. Then he said, as if he excused the situation to himself:

"The Corburys are also of ancient lineage?"

"They go back as far as Henry VIII," Fenella said quickly.

"Before that," Sir Nicolas corrected. "There was a Corbury at the Battle of Agincourt."

"Oh, was there?" Fenella exclaimed with interest. "You must tell Periquine! I am sure he would be delighted."

"I find people are sadly uninterested in their family trees," Sir Nicolas replied. "To me breeding is of the utmost import."

"I can believe that," Fenella said hoping she did not sound sarcastic. "At the same time, Sir Nicolas, you must realise that we are all descended from Adam."

He looked at her in astonishment.

"What do you mean by that?"

"Well, it is obvious is it not?" Fenella asked. "Unless men descended like angels from the skies or came up like devils from down below, every man and woman on earth today must have originated from the first man and woman, whoever they may be."

She saw that the idea which she had put forward to divert him had certainly succeeded. Sir Nicolas tapped his quizzing-glass against his teeth and then sat down in an arm-chair.

"I must have time to think about this most interesting contention of yours, Miss Lambert," he said. "I must admit it had never occurred to me before, but now I see there is a certain reasoning in what you say."

"What is more important than breeding," Fenella continued, "are brains and bravery. Every family which has been ennobled and knighted have originally received their title for some deed of valour or service in Statesmanship. We should bring up our children to strive to better themselves, not to be content with what they have inherited from their dead ancestors."

She saw a look almost of astonishment in Sir Nicolas's eyes, and thought that perhaps she was being unkind. His family tree must be, she thought, very precious to him.

It was his hobby, his consuming interest, something which he had made peculiarly his own, and now she was trying to belittle it to him.

"I hope one day, Sir Nicolas," she said quickly, "I shall have the opportunity of seeing your family tree."

"I would like to show it to you," he answered, "but I do not suppose you would find it very interesting. Genealogical tables are quite difficult to understand and most people have no conception of what they mean."

"As a matter of fact I do understand them," Fenella smiled. "Some years ago my father was working on ours. He is very fond of research, he made me help him, and I discovered some quite fascinating ancestors who I had no idea existed. One was a very wicked Austrian Princess who set the whole Court in a twitter by her scandalous misdemeanour."

"Austrian!" Sir Nicolas exclaimed. "That would account, Miss Lambert, for the colour of your hair."

Fenella looked at him questioningly and he said:

"Did you not realise that the Austrian women, especially those who live in Vienna, are famous for their very dark red hair?"

"And so I have inherited it down the ages!" Fenella cried, "what a wonderful thought! And perhaps I have also inherited some of the Princess's more reprehensible qualities."

She looked at Sir Nicolas challengingly as she spoke.

"I should have thought that unlikely," he said dryly.

"Did you have any surprises when you were researching for your family tree?" Fenella asked.

She looked surreptitiously at the clock as she spoke. She was finding it hard to keep Sir Nicolas engaged and she was hoping that Hetty and Periquine would not be long.

Surely, she thought, Hetty would be expected to return home at a reasonable time?

It was obvious that Sir Nicolas on enquiring at the Hall where she was, had been told that she was visiting Mrs. Buckle, the supposedly ill House-Keeper at the Priory.

But nearly two hours in which to make a visit of mercy would strain the credibility of even the most doting parent.

"Yes, I discovered several extremely interesting characters, among my mother's ancestors who were the Earls of St. Quentine," Sir Nicolas was saying. "The Emperor Charlemagne was one and one of the Habsburg Kings was another. Now I think of it, there is a faint chance, Miss Lambert, that we might be related."

"That would be very exciting," Fenella said. "If you ever come here again I might get our family tree from Papa and bring it for your perusal."

"I should like that," Sir Nicolas said and she realised he was speaking quite sincerely.

"Tell me about the Habsburg King whose blood we may both have in our veins," Fenella pleaded.

"Unfortunately there is not a great deal known about him . . ." Sir Nicolas began.

Because she was really curious Fenella was leaning forward intently, when suddenly the door of the Salon opened and Hetty and Lord Corbury appeared together.

There was a little silence and quite unexpectedly Fenella felt guilty, as if she were doing something wrong.

Perhaps it was the annoyance in Hetty's eyes or the expression in Lord Corbury's. She was not certain. She only knew it brought her swiftly to her feet as with a little exclamation Hetty hurried forward with both hands outstretched.

"Sir Nicolas! You have arrived at last," she exclaimed. "We had almost given up hope of ever seeing you."

"I was unfortunately delayed," Sir Nicolas replied taking both Hetty's hands in his, but raising only one to his lips.

"But now at last you are here and I am overcome with chagrin to think I was not waiting at home for you, as I have been every day this week."

"You should not have put yourself out on my account," Sir Nicolas said.

He spoke politely, but Fenella thought with a little smile that that was exactly what he did expect. He must have been quite annoyed to find on his arrival that Hetty was not waiting for him.

"How do you do, Waringham," Lord Corbury said and it was quite obvious from his tone of voice and the manner in which he held out his hand that he was definitely not pleased to see Sir Nicolas.

"The servants told me on my arrival that Hetty had come here," Sir Nicolas explained, "and as it was such a short distance I drove on in search of her."

"And now you have found me!" Hetty exclaimed. "How delightful it is to think that you will be our guest! Papa and Mama have been so looking forward to entertaining you."

Sir Nicolas's eyes were on her lovely face before he answered slowly:

"I hope you too have been looking forward to my visit."

"I have indeed," Hetty smiled, "and I have many plans of ways of amusing ourselves. Come, we must go home."

She turned as she spoke, and then as if she saw Fenella for the first time she said with a sharp note in her voice:

"Really, Fenella, you look a sad romp, and surely it is time you had a new gown. The one you have on has certainly done its duty through the years."

There was a look in Hetty's beautiful blue eyes which told Fenella that the reason for her attack lay in the fact that she and Sir Nicolas had appeared quite at home together when Hetty had first come into the room.

She was wondering how she could answer when Lord Corbury said almost roughly:

"You know as well as I do, Hetty, my Cousin Lionel spends all his money on books and there is none to spare for Fenella. New gowns, although you may not be aware of it, cost money."

Fenella knew from a note in his voice that he was not really defending her but hating Sir Nicolas because he was rich and because Hetty had been so warm in her greeting of him.

"Poor Fenella, I had forgotten!" Hetty said in a somewhat affected tone.

She held out her hand to Lord Corbury.

"Goodbye, Periquine, it is delightful to find you home again and so unexpectedly. I know Mama and Papa will want to ask you over to dinner one evening. Papa was saying only yesterday he wondered when you would return."

She turned her head towards Sir Nicolas and added:

"Periquine and I were brought up together as children, but since he left the Army he has been having a gay time in London and the country now has little fascination for him."

"That is where you are mistaken," Lord Corbury corrected. "When you are in Sussex I find it the most fascinating place in the world."

Fenella drew in her breath. She knew that Periquine was deliberately asserting himself to show Sir Nicolas that he too was a suitor for Hetty's hand, and she was afraid that Hetty would not be pleased at his being so outspoken.

But Hetty was used to having every man who looked into her lovely face a slave to her beauty.

"Dear Periquine, you were always so flattering," she simpered.

Then slipping her arm through Sir Nicolas's she looked up into his eyes and said confidingly:

"Take me away, Sir Nicolas, or Periquine will turn my head with his compliments. I swear he has a touch of the Irish in him, for he expends his blarney on every pretty girl he meets."

Lord Corbury's lips were pressed tightly together and his chin squared. Fenella saw the flash of anger in his eyes, and fearing that he would make things worse for himself, she said hastily:

"Goodbye, Hetty, you look lovely, simply lovely! I am sure that not only Periquine but every man in Sussex would vote you the most beautiful girl in the world, if they had the opportunity to do so."

As she finished speaking she realised that Sir Nicolas was smiling at her. Not a very broad smile it was true, little more than a stiff stretching of his lips, but nevertheless a smile of understanding.

"Perhaps he is more perceptive than he appears," she thought to herself.

Then with a flutter of her blue skirts Hetty led the way from the Salon into the Hall, chattering to Sir Nicolas and leaning on his arm as they walked towards the front door.

Because there was nothing else for them to do, Lord Corbury and Fenella followed behind.

"It is almost like a wedding procession," Fenella thought to herself and realised how infuriated Periquine would be if she said the words aloud.

Outside in the drive there were two vehicles, both drawn by magnificent horse-flesh.

Hetty's chaise, which she often drove herself, had only one horse but Sir Nicolas, having come from London, had a Phaeton drawn by four.

It was clear that he had changed horses on the way, because the team he had now were still spirited, still chafing at their bits, fidgeting and anxious to move off.

"Will you come with me?" Sir Nicolas asked Hetty.

"But of course," she answered.

He helped her into the Phaeton before he walked round to the other side and climbing into the driver's seat took the reins from his groom.

Towering like a Queen above them Hetty made a graceful gesture with her gloved hand.

"Goodbye, Periquine, goodbye Fenella," she said, "I hope I shall see you both again soon."

Then Sir Nicolas started his horses, and with the wheels of the Phaeton scrunching on the loose gravel they drove away down the avenue of oak trees.

"Curse him!" Lord Corbury said furiously as Fenella stood watching them out of sight. "How can I compete with a man who can afford horses like that?"

"One does not love anyone for their horses," Fenella replied.

"But Hetty cannot help being impressed with them," Lord Corbury answered. "And she is impressed with him anyway."

"He is very stiff," Fenella said, "but I think if he relaxed he might be quite interesting."

"Interesting! That stuck-up, stuffed pelican!" Lord Corbury ejaculated. "And what in God's name were you saying to him when we came into the room?"

"I was trying to keep him from coming in search of Hetty," Fenella answered. "I did not think you would want him bursting upon you in the arbour."

"How did you know we were in the arb—?" Lord Corbury began. Then added: "Blast it, Fenella, you know too much! It was bad luck his turning up after all. I was beginning to think that Hetty had forgotten his very existence."

He walked back into the house and Fenella followed him.

It was always the same, she thought: after Hetty had been at the Priory she left Periquine frustrated and unhappy.

"Did you not enjoy your time together?" she asked in a small voice.

"Of course I did," Lord Corbury answered.

They had reached the Salon by now and she saw him glance at the Priest's Hole as if he wanted to reassure himself that the money was still there.

"She is the most beautiful creature," he went on almost as if he spoke to himself. "I cannot believe there has ever been anyone as lovely. So how can I expect her to live in this squalor?"

"She has money of her own," Fenella suggested.

"I do not intend to live on my wife," Lord Corbury said harshly, "and, what is more, Hetty spends every penny that her father allows her. I could hardly expect her to pay for the food she eats or the servants who wait on her in my house."

He sounded so irritable that Fenella could only murmur apologetically:

"No, of course not."

"I must have some money," Lord Corbury said, "and, Fenella, last night I had an idea."

"An idea?" Fenella enquired.

"I was looking around the house," Lord Corbury said, "trying to find anything—even a piece of china which had been forgotten and might prove valuable— then in the attics I found these."

He went to the drawer of the desk as he spoke and brought out two black masks.

"What are they?" Fenella asked curiously.

"Masks," he said, "that were worn at a Charade

my mother arranged one Christmas. It was years ago, I was only ten at the time, so I imagine you were too young to be present."

"I certainly was at the age of four," Fenella smiled.

"I remember it well," Lord Corbury said. "I was only allowed to watch, but my father was the hero and he was a Highwayman."

"Highwayman!" Fenella exclaimed.

"The play was called 'Your Money Or Your Life,'" Lord Corbury explained.

His eyes met Fenella's as he spoke and for a moment they looked at each other.

"It would not be safe," Fenella said. "You know that most people have a footman on their coaches carrying a blunderbuss."

"Not all of them," Lord Corbury corrected, "and not in a part of the country they know well or when they are only travelling a short distance."

"Periquine . . ." Fenella began.

"We would not go on the main highway," Lord Corbury continued, "but keep to the side roads. I am sure the coaches there are not armed any more than I should carry a firearm if I was visiting your father or going to The Hall."

"No of course not," Fenella agreed.

"We could ride about five to six miles away where we would not be known. I believe that the Gentlemen of the Road, as they called, make a fortune."

"I doubt if they can collect as much as we did the other night," Fenella said.

"It is certainly more sporting," Lord Corbury continued "I have an aversion, Fenella, to creeping into a man's house when it is dark, stealing his gold when he has not a chance of defending himself or see who the intruder might be."

"We do not want to be identified," Fenella protested.

"No of course not," Lord Corbury agreed. "But at the same time it is a question of man to man, and the strongest wins, even if he does hold a pistol in one hand."

"I see what you mean," Fenella said. "All right, Periquine, when do we start?"

He held out the mask towards her.

"Why not now?"

"Now!"

Fenella took the mask from him and realised that its design, with only narrow slits for the eyes, made it a good disguise for the face, not like the frivolus wide-eyed masks that were used at Cotillions or fancy-dress parties.

"I was thinking about it in the night," Lord Corbury went on. "I reckon the best time to be on the road would be when people are going out to dinner. To begin with the woman would have their jewels on and a man would doubtless be carrying a heavy purse."

"I am sure you are right," Fenella agreed but a little apprehensively.

"We will keep in the shadows of the trees," he continued, "and assess the coach very carefully before we make a move. Then, if we think it safe, I will hold them up and you will keep your pistol trained on the coachmen while I take the goods from the occupants of the carriage."

"It sounds easy," Fenella said.

"And ought to prove quite lucrative!" Lord Corbury enthused. "That is what is important. If it is not going to prove profitable, then there is no point our risking our necks."

"They hang Highwaymen up on the gibbet at the cross-road," Fenella said.

"And they hang robbers at Tyburn," Lord Corbury retorted. "I have a suspicion that the place is not particularly important when it is your neck that is being stretched."

Fenella laughed.

"I have a feeling, Periquine, that you were not born to be hanged."

"My tutor at Eton had quite a different idea,"

Lord Corbury replied. "But if we get some really good hauls, Fenella, we should be getting on towards our goal."

"Yes of course," Fenella agreed.

She wondered what Hetty would think if she knew the risks Periquine was taking in his efforts to win her.

Would she be touched and flattered that a man gambled his life so that he could lay the spoils of his ill-gotten gains at her feet?

Or would she merely be shocked and think it reprehensible that he should not behave like a gentleman, even if he were a poverty-stricken one?

She could not answer the question. She only knew that whatever Periquine wished her to do with him she would do.

There was a light of adventure in his eyes and he was smiling. She knew that anything was better than seeing him depressed, miserable and without hope.

"One good thing," she said, "is that I discovered upstairs, also in the attic as it happens, the riding-breeches you wore when you were fifteen. Your mother was a hoarder, Periquine, and there are all sorts of things up there put away carefully, which now quite surprisingly are coming into use."

"Riding-breeches!" Lord Corbury exclaimed. "Well, you certainly cannot come dressed as a woman."

"I will go and put them on," Fenella said, "and if I tuck my hair under one of your riding-caps, I promise you I shall look at a most ferocious Highwayman."

She turned the mask over in her hands.

"This only covers the upper part of our faces," she said. "I believe that Highwaymen always wear a black scarf which they can pull up over their chins. That means only their mouths can be seen and it is very difficult to recognise a person by their mouth only."

"You are right," Lord Corbury cried. "I have a scarf somewhere which will be just what we need. And anyway I will wear my oldest clothes."

Fenella was just going to say that she thought however old his clothes he would look extremely elegant in them, because with his good figure, it was difficult for him to look anything else. Then she decided it was best for him to take a lot of trouble to disguise himself.

She could not help feeling that if she saw Periquine however well he was masked she would recognize him.

There was something about his broad shoulders and narrow hips, the manner in which he walked and sat a horse, the carriage of his head and his whole lithe athletic body which made him different from other men.

Very different indeed from Sir Nicolas. Different too, she was sure, from the majority of his contemporaries.

Yet there was no use in splitting straws. Periquine was intent on this escapade and although she was a little doubtful of its being successful, she knew that any arguments she might present were not likely to prove effective.

Every time he saw Hetty it made him more anxious to marry her and more infuriated with his impecunious position.

The five thousand pounds they had left from their robbery were not going to last for ever. In fact Fenella had the feeling that Periquine would soon spend it, not on riotus living, but on the sheer necessities of everyday existence at the Priory.

'We have to have some money somehow,' she thought to herself as she went upstairs thinking of what lay ahead.

It was true quite a lot of Highwaymen were hanged, but at the same time there were undoubtedly a large number of them still at large. She could only hope they would be lucky.

She gave a little sigh.

"And if we fail . . . we fail together," she whispered to herself. "I do not mind hanging if I am hanged beside Periquine."

Chapter Four

It was a misty evening with a promise of rain and the small wood seemed dark and drear.

Lord Corbury however was in high spirits and Fenella could not help thinking he looked a romantic figure with his black mask and a black silk handkerchief lying on his chest ready to be pulled up over his chin.

"What do you wager we will take in our first haul?" he asked.

"If they are carrying many valuables, they will undoubtedly do their best to protect them," Fenella replied.

"Still afraid that I shall have a piece of lead blown through me?" he asked mockingly.

"I am sure that having survived the war your luck will remain proverbial," she replied. But she wished she felt a little more optimistic in herself.

It seemed to her a really foolhardy adventure with nothing planned, with no knowledge of what they were up against, and however much she might try to ignore it the shadow of the gibbet lay over the whole escapade.

Lord Corbury was riding a stallion which was such a fine piece of horseflesh that Fenella felt nervously it was an animal that no-one would be likely to forget.

And she herself in riding-breeches was astride

a roan on which her father had expended quite a considerable sum.

He never economised where horseflesh was concerned, or indeed when it came to anything that appertained to his own comfort.

His only economies, Fenella thought a little bitterly, lay in feminine fancies and her own in particular.

Lord Corbury's horse was a little restive despite the fact that they had ridden for over an hour to reach their present destination.

He had chosen the place because although it was not on a highway, it was on a fairly frequented road lying between several large estates whose owners were of local importance and most likely to be entertaining.

"Someone will be giving a dinner-party," he said confidently, "and the ladies should be wearing tiaras, necklaces and rings worth a fortune."

"Have you thought how you will dispose of them?" Fenella asked.

"Doubtless someone will be able to give us the required information," he answered. "If not, we can always ask our friend Isaac Goldstein."

Fenella knew that he was teasing her, but at the same time she could not help exclaiming:

"Really, Periquine, you have no sense of propriety!"

"That is a fault I usually find in you!" he retorted.

Then when she was trying to think of an answer, he said:

"There is a coach coming!"

They could see for nearly a mile down the road. It was bordered only by low hedges, green with spring buds.

Fenella perceived a coach moving towards them at what she judged was a quite respectable pace.

There were no outriders, but there were two men on the box, a coachman who as he grew nearer she saw was an old man, and a footman who appeared young and slim but certainly not athletic.

They were both dressed in a dark blue livery with polished buttons and three-cornered hats.

As the coach drew nearer, they could see it was slightly old-fashioned, but obviously it had been expensive and its owner's crest was emblazoned on the panels of the door.

Lord Corbury had watched its approach in silence. Now he glanced at Fenella and said with a note of excitement in his voice:

"Here goes! Keep close behind me."

They spurred their horses down to the road-side, and as the coach drew level with them Lord Corbury pulled the black handkerchief over his chin and levelled his pistol.

"Stand and deliver!" he cried in what Fenella knew was intended to be a ferocious voice.

It certainly had an effect. The old coachman with an audible gasp pulled his horses to a standstill, while the young footman with a shrill scream put both hands high above his head.

"Lawks a mercy, don't shoot! Don't shoot Oi', Sir," he cried.

"Nobody is going to shoot you if you stay quiet as you are," Lord Corbury replied.

He glanced at Fenella who had come up beside him and was keeping her pistol trained on the two men on the box. He then dismounted from his horse and handed her the bridle before he pulled open the door of the carriage, still with his pistol in his hand.

This, Fenella knew, was the dangerous moment. The delay had given the gentleman, if there was one inside, time to draw and if necessary load a pistol.

Lord Corbury looked inside the carriage. In the far corner there was a very old man. His hair was dead white, his eyes were closed, and it was obvious he was asleep.

Sitting beside him was a Lady. Extremely pretty, she could not have been much more than thirty years of age. Her hair was dark and elegantly arranged high on her head. In it sparkled a large tiara of emeralds and diamonds.

Round her neck there was an emerald necklace, and bracelets to match were clasped round her thin wrists.

Lord Corbury stared at her for a moment. Then still in his assumed voice he said gruffly:

"Hand over your valuables and quickly."

The Lady turned towards the sleeping man and touched him on the arm.

"Your purse, George!" she said softly. "Give me your purse, dear."

The old Gentleman woke up with a start.

"Purse? Purse? You want me to pay? Where are we? At the toll gate?"

"No dear, this . . . er . . . Gentleman requires your money."

"Of course, of course, it is here somewhere."

He fumbled uncertainly in the inside of his evening-coat and finally drew a long purse from the pocket of his satin knee-breeches.

The Lady took it from him and handed it to Lord Corbury. As she did so the old Gentleman closed his eyes and composed himself once again for slumber.

"My husband does not see very well," she said as if she felt an explanation was needed.

"And now your jewels," Lord Corbury demanded.

Her dark eyes looked at him as she hesitated. Then she said in a low voice:

"Please . . . please do not take them! They are all I have. They mean so much to me. I will give you anything . . . anything you like . . . rather than part with my emeralds."

There was a moment's silence before Lord Corbury said in his normal voice with a hint of laughter in it:

"Anything?"

Her eyes flickered for a moment and there was a little smile on her red lips.

"Anything within . . . reason," she replied softly.

Lord Corbury pulled the black handkerchief down from his chin. He too was smiling as he bent towards the red mouth which was only a few inches away from him.

She made no effort to evade what was obviously inevitable. In fact she leant forward and as Lord Corbury's lips held hers captive her hand crept round his neck to hold him closer still.

It was a long kiss, a passionate one, and Fenella watching suddenly felt a sharp pain as if a dagger had been stabbed into her body.

Her pistol was pointing at the coachman, but she could not take her eyes from the couple locked together in a close embrace just inside the carriage.

They were only a few feet away from her, and she had never in her life known such agony as it was to watch Periquine kissing another woman.

She had heard him making love to Hetty, she had known what they were doing when every afternoon they disappeared into the arbour, but thinking about it was not the same as actually seeing it taking place in front of her.

She knew in that moment she would give up her hope of Heaven if only Periquine would kiss her in such a manner.

The bend of his head, the manner in which his arm had gone round the woman he was kissing, and the way she could see their lips moving passionately against each other's was somehow beyond all her imaginings.

She felt as if she could not breathe, and the pain in her body seemed to increase every second that passed.

It was as if time had stood still and she had watched Periquine kiss this stranger for hours, before finally they drew apart from each other.

"You are very sweet," Lord Corbury said and his voice was hoarse.

"And you are very . . . persuasive for a . . . Highwayman."

They were looking at each other and Lord Corbury was obviously making no effort to leave, when Fenella looking down the road saw in the distance a vehicle approaching.

"There is someone coming," she said sharply.

It seemed to her that her voice was unnaturally loud so that it rang out like a clarion.

As if it recalled Lord Corbury to a realisation of his somewhat precarious position, he stepped back from the coach and shut the door.

"Goodbye, fair Charmer," he said, "perhaps one day we shall meet again."

"I hope so . . . I very much hope so," the Lady replied softly.

Fenella lowered her pistol.

"Drive on," she said hoping that now her voice sounded gruff and masculine.

But even if it did not she was certain the men on the box were too worried and bewildered to think of anything but their own plight.

Nervously, as if he could hardly believe that nothing worse was going to happen to him, the young footman lowered his arms. The coachman jerked on his reins, the wheels started to turn and the coach moved off.

The Lady inside bent forward, her eyes on Lord Corbury, and she waved until they could no longer see her.

As if she could not bear to watch the coach any longer, Fenella spurred her horse and rode back into the wood.

Here she pulled off her mask, untied the black handkerchief from round her neck and stuffed it into her pocket.

She had just finished when Lord Corbury joined her.

He was holding the purse in his hand and as he drew his horse to a standstill he jingled it and remarked ironically:

"It does not seem over-heavy."

"Do you know who that was?" Fenella asked, and her tone was terse because she was angry.

"No, who was it?" Lord Corbury asked eagerly.

"That is old Squire Enslow," Fenella replied. "He is enormously wealthy, and I imagine that is his fourth wife, whom he married about three years ago. I can assure you, if the County gossip is to be believed, that her emeralds are by no means all she possesses. They say she leads the Squire by the nose and has extorted more out of him than all his other three wives put together."

Lord Corbury laughed.

"Then she deserves every penny of it! A pretty wench like that tied to an old dogger is a crime against nature."

"You were supposed to be a Highwayman," Fenella said and thought to herself that her voice sounded peevish.

"I think it would definitely be worthwhile to pursue the acquaintance of Mrs. Enslow," Lord Corbury said as if speaking to himself. "I wonder how we can persuade her to visit the Priory."

"And put your head in a noose," Fenella asked. "Do you think that if she recognises you, which she will undoubtedly do if you meet again, she will keep such an amusing tale to herself?"

Lord Corbury did not speak and Fenella continued.

"The noble owner of the Priory masquerading as a Highwayman and robbing travellers would be a scandal which would involve serious repercussions on your social standing, if nothing worse."

Lord Corbury sighed.

"Perhaps you are right," he said. "All the same, she was a pretty piece."

"And her emeralds which you bartered for a kiss are worth thousands," Fenella snapped.

Lord Corbury was not listening to her. He was turning the contents of the purse out into his open palm.

"Ten—no eleven sovereigns," he said.

He looked up and saw the expression on Fenella's face.

"Not worth the risk," he said quietly.

"Undoubtedly not!" Fenella replied.

He looked at her for a moment, then he pulled off his mask and threw it away into the bushes.

"You are right, Fenella, you are always right," he said, "but it was rather fun all the same. Come on, let us go home."

He put out his hand as he spoke, and after a moment's hesitation she put hers in it.

He squeezed her fingers.

"You are not angry with me?"

There was a beguiling note in his voice which she could not resist.

"No, Periquine," she answered.

But as they rode back towards the Priory Fenella told herself that, while she was not angry, the sight of Periquine kissing another woman had made her acknowledge a truth which she had been trying to evade for the last week.

The truth was that she loved him, not as a child, not with the close cousinly love which had been theirs ever since she could remember, but as a woman loves a man.

She loved him, she loved him! She loved everything about him, except of course the fact that he was not in love with her.

They rode swiftly because, now the adventure was over, Lord Corbury was in a hurry to get home.

The sound of their horses' hoofs galloping over the fields seemed to fall into a certain rhythm which Fenella could not escape.

"I love him . . . I love him . . . I love him . . ."

The words repeated themselves over and over in her mind, but she knew there was nothing different in her heart from what had always been there.

She had loved him as a child and she had counted the hours until he returned from school.

She had loved him when she had agonised over him night after night during the war, and she had loved him from the moment she had heard his voice in the Salon making love to Hetty Baldwyn while she was hidden in the Priest's Hole.

"I suppose that being with a man who is so handsome, so attractive, so adorable in every way," she told herself, "it was inevitable that I should fall hopelessly in love with him."

But for Periquine it was very different. There was a whole world of beautiful women for him to choose from.

While Hetty might be too spoilt to contemplate marriage where there was not enough money, she was at least prepared to hold him captive with her beauty and in addition to allow him liberties which Fenella suspected she would not grant to her other suitors. But then who was likely to resist Periquine?

She looked at him riding beside her. He was far the best-looking man she had ever seen. And even in his old clothes he had an elegance that was unmistakable. Perhaps the right word—was "a presence" which other men of his age did not have.

He turned to smile at her and she felt her heart turn over in her breast.

"You look a ragamuffin in those clothes," he said. "You had best let me take your horse round to the stables while you change. I cannot think what the grooms would say if they saw you."

"I expect they would merely remark that Master Periquine had been up to his tricks again," Fenella said.

"Put up to them no doubt by Miss Fenella!" Lord Corbury finished.

And they were both laughing as they reached the door of the Priory.

Three days later Sir Nicolas Waringham walked in through the front door of the Priory without troubling to ring the bell.

By this time he had learnt it was broken and even if it had not been, it was doubtful if anyone would have answered it.

He put his hat and gloves down on the Hall-table and then started a systematic search of the rooms. He found them all empty, until delving into the kitchen quarters he discovered Fenella in what was known as "the laundry" ironing a number of cravats on a deal table.

She looked up as she heard his footsteps on the flagged floor and exclaimed:

"Sir Nicolas, you are very early!"

"Hetty has gone shopping in Brighton," he answered, "and I suspicioned that Corbury would be out riding."

"He has gone to look at his farms which are being repaired," Fenella answered. "Do you want to see him?"

"I do not," Sir Nicolas replied, "I want to talk to you."

Fenella was not surprised. She had realised that during Sir Nicolas's visits over the past days regarding his Family Tree, they had ranged over a number of other subjects, and she would not have been feminine had she been unaware that he was intrigued by her.

She knew it was because she was so different from any other female that he had met in the past.

For one thing she was not "setting her cap at him" and she treated him easily and without formality. She made no particular effort to entertain him, nor did she appear awe-struck by his condescension.

Actually Fenella had found Sir Nicolas surprisingly interesting.

She learnt that he had done an amazing amount of intricate and quite enthralling research on his own family tree and also on those of a number of other noble families.

What was more, he was well read and well informed, and as she had guessed on their first acquaintance he was far more perceptive about other people than he appeared at first acquaintance.

She had begun to believe that his stiffness and pomposity was a kind of armour with which he girded himself against the world.

She anticipated that one day she would learn the secret as to why he behaved in such a manner and why at times he seemed determined to antagonise other people by asserting his superiority.

There was however no pretence about him at the moment. He sat on the edge of the large table and watched Fenella goffering the frill of Lord Corbury's cravat.

"May I inquire if there is no-one else to do that for you?" he enquired.

"Of course there is not," Fenella replied, "not with a dinner-party planned for this evening, and old Barnes hurrying round like a scatty hen forgetting where he has put the knives and forks!"

She fetched another iron from the fire and said:

"That Hetty should wish to dine here has caused us an inordinate amount of trouble. Whose idea was it anyway?"

"Mine, as a matter of fact."

"Yours!" Fenella exclaimed. "But why? Why should you want to have a bad dinner at the Priory when you could be entertained royally at the Hall?"

"I wanted to see you," he answered.

"To see me!" Fenella echoed, and then she began to laugh.

"Why are you laughing?" he enquired. "I planned it very carefully. Hetty is to be chaperoned by her brother and you and Corbury will make us five. Not an ideal number, but I cannot see any point in inviting an outsider."

Fenella was still laughing.

"So it was your idea! Well, Sir Nicolas, you are in for a surprise."

"Why?" he enquired.

"Because," Fenella answered, "although I shall be here you will not see me."

He stared at her, realising this was some kind of puzzle to which he should find an answer.

"I must be very obtuse," he said after a moment.

"I suppose I shall have to tell you," Fenella said, her eyes twinkling mischievously, "so let me

ask you another question. Who, Sir Nicolas, did you
think is going to cook the dinner?"

Her words made him start and he said almost
incredulously:

"You do not mean, that you . . ."

"Of course," Fenella answered. "Who else is
there?"

She laughed again and then said as if she was
speaking to a small child:

"The trouble with you, Sir Nicolas, is you do not
understand the problems of ordinary people. You are
so wealthy you have no idea that everything, and
especially servants, cost money. As you should have
realised by now, the only people in the house are
old Barnes who is well over seventy and Mrs. Buckle
who does her best but cannot possibly cope with this
big house or for that matter with Periquine's appetite?"

"But surely Corbury is not as impoverished as all
that?" Sir Nicolas ejaculated.

"I should have thought you would have realised
by now that Periquine does not wish to have the
house falling about his ears, that he would prefer to
have a Butler and footmen in the hall to let you in
when you arrive, and he does not enjoy seeing the
curtains full of holes and carpets so threadbare one
catches one's foot in them."

Fenella spoke almost crossly.

She felt she could understand why Periquine resented Sir Nicolas with his enormous wealth and that
when he was at the Priory, although he might not
intend it, he made verything look shabbier and more
threadbare.

There was a moment's pause and then Sir Nicolas
said:

"I am sorry, Fenella, I did not think."

"That is just the trouble," Fenella replied. "It is
not a case of the rich not caring, they just do not
visualise the problems that other people have to
face."

Sir Nicolas was silent for a moment and then he
said:

"It is quite easy, I will arrange everything."

"What do you mean by that?" Fenella asked.

She spoke rather absently as if she were not really interested because she had just noticed a hole in one of Periquine's cravats.

A number of them were getting old, she realised, and although he had a fairly good supply they were undoubtedly expensive and it would be difficult to replace those that would soon be past being worn.

"I travel," Sir Nicolas said, "with two valets, two coachmen and two grooms. My second valet and my second groom are both trained to wait at table. They will be here this evening.

"My head valet who has been with me for many years is a first-class Chef. I had him taught when he was quite young so that, when I went abroad or journeyed North, I should not suffer any inconvenience if we were forced to stay at Inns where the food is usually inedible."

Fenella put down her iron and stared at him wide-eyed.

"What are you suggesting?"

"I am not suggesting," Sir Nicolas said. "I am informing you that everything will be seen to this evening and you will entertain me at dinner as I planned you should do."

"And what do you think Periquine will say to that?" Fenella asked. "After all, this is his house."

"I can hardly believe that Corbury, selfish and egotistical though he may be," Sir Nicolas said curtly, "will insist on your cooking his dinner as if you were a servant, when there is a reasonable alternative."

He paused and added:

"Indeed I very much doubt if he will even notice the change in plan. For I am quite convinced you have not told him what you intend to do."

This was the truth and Fenella could not contradict it. She was however surprised that Sir Nicolas should have such an insight into the relationship between herself and her cousin.

"Is what you . . . suggest really . . . possible?" she asked hesitatingly.

"It is not only possible," Sir Nicolas replied, "it is what is going to take place. Have you planned the menu?"

"Yes of course," Fenella said. "It is rather simple, not the luxurious dishes to which you are used."

"My man will produce those in which he excels and which he knows I prefer," Sir Nicolas said. "He will also bring all the necessary ingredients. You can leave everything in his hands. He will be over immediately after luncheon."

Fenella took the irons away from the fire and picked up the crisp white cravats.

"I suppose I ought to say thank you," she said, "but you have taken my breath away. I am not used to having everything managed for me."

Even as she spoke she wished that Periquine would be as positive and perhaps as masterful.

"It is having money," she thought, "knowing you only have to give a command and it is carried out. Knowing there are always people paid to obey one's orders."

At the same time she knew that in truth she was relieved that she would not have to cook the dinner and perhaps have Hetty learn later that she had done so.

She knew how easy it would be for the spoilt Beauty to sneer and make fun of her slavish devotion to Periquine, and for him to be embarrassed by it. There was always the possibility that Hetty would make him feel awkward and perhaps ashamed of imposing on her.

She felt in some ways that she should refuse to allow Sir Nicolas to interfere, and yet his plan seemed to make everything so easy.

As they walked from the laundry back along the passage towards the Salon, Fenella said:

"What did you really want to see me about this morning?"

She had an idea that they had been talking of something the day before and Sir Nicolas had now dropped in to speak further about it. But she could not think what it was and wanted him to remind her.

"Do I have to have an excuse?" Sir Nicolas enquired.

Fenella looked at him quickly. She could not believe that he really came to see her just for herself.

She was aware that he liked talking to her about his genealogical interests. But she supposed that since there was no-one else that he could converse with in such a manner, anyone was better than no-one.

Nevertheless he was Hetty's suitor, and the fact that he was staying on at the Hall rather longer than had been anticipated was surely an indication that sooner or later he would declare himself.

In which case there was every likelihood that Sir Virgil would accept him enthusiastically as his future son-in-law.

Fenella did not answer Sir Nicolas's question. Instead she put the cravats down on a chair in the hall ready for her to take them upstairs to Periquine's bed-room, and led the way to the Salon.

"I ought to offer you some refreshment," she said, "and as a matter of fact there is some wine in the house, because Periquine bought it for the dinner party tonight."

"Is the cellar really empty?" Sir Nicolas enquired in a voice which told Fenella that to him it was an unheard-of contingency.

"Completely," she answered, "but do not tell Augustus so. If you do, he is certain to say that the port is not mature enough for him, and that will annoy Periquine."

Hetty's brother Augustus Baldwyn was a man for whom Fenella had an almost violent dislike.

He had always been odious as a child, and now that he was grown-up he made it a practice to ogle every young woman under the age of forty and to boast volubly of his success to anyone who would listen to him.

"I will certainly not do anything which would upset you," Sir Nicolas said. "And I am sorry, Fenella, that this dinner-party should have caused so much commotion. I had no idea when I suggested it to Hetty what it would entail."

Fenella did not retort that more than likely Hetty also welcomed it as an opportunity of seeing Periquine.

Since Sir Nicolas's arrival she had not been able to get away so often to visit the Priory, even presuming she had wished to do so, with the result that Periquine had been on edge and ready to sink into the dismals when the day passed without a sight of her.

"You are not to apologise," Fenella said. "It is not your fault that things are as they are. But try to remember that Periquine is below hatches and please, whatever you do, do not suggest any gaming after dinner. You know how that odious Augustus always tries to win from people who cannot afford it."

"He does not win from me," Sir Nicolas replied.

"Then I am glad you are too clever for him," Fenella said. "He is always proclaiming that he wins thousands of pounds a year. And although frankly I do not believe him, it infuriates me to hear him talk in such a bumptious manner."

"Shall I prevent him from coming tonight?" Sir Nicolas said with what was for him quite a broad smile.

"I wish you could," Fenella said, "but Hetty must have a chaperon. Sir Virgil's aspirations would be all too obvious if he allowed you to escort her alone in a closed carriage after dark."

She spoke without thinking and added quickly:

"I am sorry, Sir Nicolas, I should not have said that."

"You can say anything you please," he answered. "That is what I most like about you. You do not pretend, and you speak the truth."

"Not always, I am afraid," Fenella said.

"I think with eyes like yours it would be difficult for you to lie," Sir Nicolas said unexpectedly.

She looked up at him and saw an expression in his face which made her feel strange, as if quite by mistake she had stumbled on something intimate and secret.

Then before she could speak or Sir Nicolas could say anything else, the door opened and Lord Corbury came bursting into the room.

"Look at this, Fenella," he shouted, "what the hell am I . . ."

Fenella saw he had a letter in his hand. Then as he realised that she was not alone and that Sir Nicolas was with her he stopped speaking.

He stiffened and with what was obviously an effort he said more quietly:

"Good morning, Waringham, I was not expecting you."

"I was just leaving," Sir Nicolas said suavely. "I called to see Miss Lambert and I must no longer encroach upon her valuable time."

As he spoke he bowed and raised Fenella's hand to his lips, before with his usual stiff dignity he walked from the room.

Lord Corbury made no effort to escort him to the front door. Instead he turned to Fenella with the letter in his hand and an almost agonized expression on his handsome face.

"Read this," he said, "read it and tell me what the devil I can do!"

Fenella took the letter from him. She saw it was written in French and was glad that she was proficient in that language.

The writing-paper smelt strongly of the fragrance of gardenias, the hand-writing was elaborate and obviously feminine.

She turned a little sideways so that the light from the window could fall on the paper, while Lord Corbury walked to the mantelpiece to stand staring in a dejected fashion into the empty fire-place.

Mon cher

I have the Greatest good News which I know will make You Happy. I am a Widow! My poor Husband passed away two months ago. I have not Written before because I have been so Busily Occupied in settling His vast Estates.

Despite the War and the deprivations from which We all suffered, He was a very rich man and His lands Overseas are still intact and in good Heart.

Everything is now Settled to the Satisfaction of the Attorneys and Myself. It is therefore with the greatest Delight Mon Cher, Periquine, that I can come to You as We planned, and We can be Married as soon as it can be arranged.

I am crossing the Channel on Wednesday 28th May and should be with You the following Day. I am not certain at which time my Ship will arrive in Dover, but I will hire a post-chaise with four good Horses as soon as I disembark and it shall carry Me with all swiftness to Your beautiful Home of which You have told Me so much. Then I shall be in Your arms and all Our problems for the future will be solved—for We shall be Together.

My heart and my Love are Yours as always.

I remain Your most Devoted and Adoring,

Amaline

Fenella read through the letter, her eyes growing wider and more surprised with every word until she reached the end.

Then she looked up at Periquine and said almost inaudibly:

"Who is she?"

"Madame D'Arbley," he replied. "I met her, of course, while I was in France."

"You love . . . her?"

"I was fond of her while I was abroad," he answered, "but I never expected her husband to die."

"You mean," Fenella said her voice growing a little stronger, "that you told her that if she was free you would wish to marry her."

Lord Corbury straightened himself.

"A man says a lot of damn silly things at certain times," he muttered.

"You mean . . . that she was . . . she was your . . . mistress?"

"Oh hell, Fenella," Lord Corbury said sharply, "what do you expect a fellow to do? When the fighting was over the only amusement within miles of where we were camped was the D'Arbley's Chateau. They were very hospitable. The Officers all fought for invitations from the alluring Amaline."

"And she fell in love with you?" Fenella asked.

"We were both somewhat infatuated," Lord Corbury replied frankly. "But I never thought there was any chance of her being free or of her taking me so seriously. Curse it, I have not heard from the woman since I left that part of France."

"You were in Belgium after Waterloo."

"And Amaline was fifty miles away."

Fenella looked down again at the letter.

"She appears very . . . determined," she said uncomfortably.

"She would be!" Lord Corbury said grimly. "The French love a title, and Amaline had often expressed her regret in no uncertain terms that her husband was not a nobleman."

"What are you going to do?" Fenella asked.

"That is what I am asking you," Lord Corbury replied. "When does she say she is arriving?"

"Wednesday, 28th . . ."

She stopped.

"Periquine, do you realise that is today? She will be here this afternoon! You cannot ask her to stay. Remember Hetty is coming to dinner this evening."

"Oh my God!"

Lord Corbury put his hand to his forehead. Then he walked across the room to stand at the window looking out into the garden.

"Help me! Fenella, help me!" he cried, "this is one of the worst jams I have ever been in."

"You do not wish to . . . marry her. . . ?" Fenella asked.

"Marry her? Of course I do not want to marry her!" Lord Corbury retorted. "It was all over and done with by the time the Regiment moved. I am not saying that she did not give me a good time and I found her very attractive. But as for marriage—she is not at all the type of woman I would want as my wife. Besides there have been—several others since."

"And now Hetty," Fenella said softly.

"If Hetty got to hear of this it would be disastrous," Lord Corbury said. "Only yesterday she asked me . . ."

He stopped as if what he was about to say was too intimate to relate even to Fenella.

"We have to think of something," Fenella said desperately.

Then Periquine's words, "There have been several others since," seemed to repeat themselves in her mind.

"Periquine, I have an idea."

"It better be a good one," he answered grimly.

"It is, I think it is very good. I must be your wife!"

Chapter Five

"My wife!" Lord Corbury echoed.

"I meant . . . that I should . . . pretend to be your . . . wife," Fenella said quickly, a faint colour coming to her cheeks as she realised he might have misunderstood what she meant.

He did not answer, and after a moment she went on:

"Do you not see, Periquine, it is the only possible way to get rid of your friend immediately? She will not want to stay if she thinks you are married, and to make quite sure she goes, I have another idea."

"What is that?" Lord Corbury asked.

"I will say someone in the house . . . one of the servants will do—has scarlet fever. It is very infectious and I cannot believe that Madame D'Arbley will wish to run the risk of catching it."

Lord Corbury stood looking at Fenella for a moment. Then he threw back his head and laughed.

"Fenella, you are incredible!" he exclaimed. "I believe you would rescue me if I had gone down into Hell itself!"

"I should do my best," Fenella answered, "since you have a genius for getting yourself into scrapes."

Lord Corbury, still laughing, shrugged his shoulders.

"What is life if we never take any risks?" he said. "But I must say I was not expecting my pigeons to come home to roost so quickly, if that is the right expression!"

"One pigeon, and of French origin," Fenella said. "Do you think she will make a great fuss?"

"What can she do if you are really convincing?" Lord Corbury asked. "After all, when I left her she was married. She could not expect me to carry a torch for her for ever."

"No, of course not," Fenella said, in a matter of fact voice. "And now let us make plans. If we are not careful, she will dismiss the Post-Chaise, and then she will be stranded here."

"That must not happen," Lord Corbury said quickly.

Fenella put her hand up to her forehead.

"What I suggest," she said, "is that I will greet her in the hall when I hear the Post-Chaise drive up to the door. You can be somewhere about, but she must not see you, and as soon as she steps in the Salon, you must stop the Post-Chaise from driving away, and tell the driver that he will be required to take his passenger back either to Dover or to London, wherever she decides to go."

"We do not know what time she will be arriving," Lord Corbury protested. "Have I got to hang about the whole afternoon?"

"I am afraid you have," Fenella said severely, "and once you have dealt with the Post-Chaise, you must come into the Salon and greet her."

"Why must I meet her? I am sure it is unnecessary!"

"Really, Periquine, you cannot be so cowardly as to leave me alone with you *chère amie* who will doubtless be incensed at the thought that you have escaped her. If you are not there, after she arrives, I swear to you I will tell her the truth, and then you can handle the situation by yourself."

"You are blackmailing me!" Lord Corbury sad accusingly.

"It may be blackmail," Fenella answered, "but I promise you I am not joking."

"All right," he capitulated, "I will do as you wish. But for God's sake get rid of her as quickly as possible, in case Hetty comes over and finds her here!"

"Hetty is not likely to call this afternoon if she is coming to dinner this evening. Of course, if you like, we can ask Madame D'Arbley to make us six . . . five is an uneven number."

There was a mischievous twinkle in Fenella's eye as she spoke. Lord Corbury picked up one of the cushions and threw it at her.

She turned aside so that it missed her head but struck the wall with some force. The old faded silk split open and a quantity of white goose-feathers fell out on to the floor.

"Really, Periquine, you are impossible!" Fenella cried. "How can you make such a mess when there is so much to do?"

"It is entirely your fault," Lord Corbury retorted. "You deliberately provoked me, and if it is a punishment to pick up all those feathers, it is one you undoubtedly deserve."

Fenella stuffed as many of the goose-feathers back into the cushion as she could and opening a drawer of an ancient oak chest, pushed it inside.

"I will mend that later," she said. "I had best go upstairs and tidy myself, just in case Madame D'Arbley arrives before we are ready for her."

She turned towards the door. Then she paused.

"Would it be very remiss of me, Periquine," she said in a somewhat embarrassed voice, "if I suggested that I should wear one of your Mama's gowns?"

For a moment Lord Corbury looked surprised, and then he glanced at what Fenella was wearing and realised, as if for the first time, how old and faded her frock was and how she had, in fact, grown out of it. It was too tight over her breasts and too narrow across the shoulders.

She saw he was staring at her and the colour rose in her cheeks.

"I would not ask such a . . . thing," she said uncomfortably, "if I did not feel Madame D'Arbley would think it very mean of you to economise so obviously on your wife's attire."

"I had no idea Mama's clothes were still here," Lord Corbury said, "but of course take what you want. I am quite certain she would approve if she knew you were getting me out of trouble."

As he spoke he gave Fenella his most irresistible smile and without speaking again she turned and left the Salon.

"He never notices what I wear," she told herself as she went up the old oak staircase. "But perhaps if I dressed like Hetty, he might even admire me."

It was a fascinating thought, but at the same time she knew that never was she likely to possess even one gown to equal the expensive, elaborate creations of which Hetty had an apparently inexhaustible supply.

"It is hard for men to realise how much clothes mean to a woman," Fenella told herself sensibly.

At the same time she could not help wishing that her Father could be more understanding, and that it was not so hurtful to realise that Periquine never really looked at her.

He accepted her, he knew when she was there, he found her useful. He obviously liked being with her, but until this moment, when she drew attention to herself, he had never noticed her.

She doubted, if he were asked, if he would be able to tell the colour of her eyes.

All Lady Corbury's clothes had been moved upstairs to the room on the second floor which had been used by her lady's-maid. On every wall there were huge wardrobes, but the dust was thick on the floor and Fenella knew that no one had entered the room for years.

She pulled back the curtains over the windows and opened one of the wardrobes. Inside there were riding-habits, cloaks, driving-coats, but no gowns.

She tried another and was greeted by a kaleidoscope of brocades, velvets and gauzes. These she realised were the evening-gowns.

But the third wardrobe was more productive. This contained Lady Corbury's day-clothes. There were quite a number of elegant dresses which Fenella realised were not too ludicrously out of date.

The fashion vogue had changed very little during the war and although Hetty's gowns were beginning to show signs of a waist and they were wider than those of six years previously when Lady Corbury had died, the difference was not startling.

It was true however that dresses were now far more elaborate, with frills, lace-rouchings, bows and braid, but such details were, Fenella thought, immaterial.

After inspecting a number of gowns in the wardrobe she chose one which she knew would make her look older. It was dark green crepe and trimed with satin ribbons and a small amount of lace round the décolletage.

Carrying it carefully over her arm so it should not touch the dusty floor, Fenella took it next door into what had been the maid's bedroom.

Here there were all the other boxes, objets d'art, brushes, combs and toilet accessories which had been brought upstairs from Lady Corbury's bedroom.

It was not difficult to find her Ladyship's jewel-case standing on the dressing-table. Fenella expected it to be empty, as she was well aware that any jewels which Lady Corbury left had been sold during her husband's long illness after she herself had died.

But in one of the small compartments there was what she was seeking for—a gold wedding ring.

That had not been sold, neither had a necklace of jet beads and two small earrings to match. As they were valueless, they had been left behind.

Fenella picked up the ring and looked at it for a moment before she slipped it on her finger.

She had the uncomfortable feeling that she was doing something wrong, but she knew that any woman in Madame D'Arbley's position would be suspicious if she noticed Lord Corbury's wife was not wearing a wedding-ring.

She felt the ring encircle the third finger on her left hand.

"Forgive me," she said, as if she were speaking to Periquine's mother. "But I have to help your son . . . he does not wish to be involved with this . . . woman and I do not suppose anyway . . . that you would wish her to be your . . . daughter-in-law. I must save him . . . he is so . . . hopeless at looking after . . . himself."

The little prayer seemed to bring Fenella a sense of peace, and the uncomfortable feeling of guilt disappeared.

She did not ask herself whether Periquine would mind her wearing his mother's wedding-ring, because she was certain that unless she drew attention to it, he would not even notice it on her finger!

Then shutting the jewel-case, and carrying the jet jewellery in her hand, Fenella went downstairs to one of the less dusty rooms to change.

The gown was rather big for her round the waist, and somewhat too long but otherwise it fitted comparatively well and, as she had hoped, made her look more mature.

She arranged her hair in curls high on the top of her head, pinning it securely and thinking with a smile it gave her both height and dignity. With the jet necklace round her neck and wearing the earrings she went downstairs.

There was no sign of Lord Corbury and finally she ran him to earth in the Gun-room.

"I shall be able to hear the Post-Chaise coming up the drive from here," he said quickly as she entered, as if he expected her to complain that he was not nearer the hall.

He was polishing the barrel of one of his guns and he did not look up as he spoke.

"I am ready," Fenella said.

He raised his head. Then gave an exclamation of surprise.

"I should not have recognised you!" he said, "you look so—respectable!"

His eyes were twinkling as he spoke, and Fenella replied:

"One more word, Periquine, and I will refuse to be the staid wife you would undoubtedly have chosen as your bride."

Lord Corbury did not answer. He was still looking at her and after a moment he said:

"I did not know you had such a white skin, Fenella. You should wear green more often."

"Your compliments overwhelm me," Fenella replied. "Do you think them up before you spring them on your lady-loves, or do they just come naturally?"

"You little vixen!" Lord Corbury exclaimed.

He stepped towards her as though he would shake her as he had done before when she had provoked him, but at that moment they heard the sound of wheels coming down the drive.

"She is coming . . . she is coming!" Fenella cried. "Now, Periquine, do not forget to hold the Post Chaise, and I only pray she believes the moonshine I am about to relate."

The sound of the Chaise drew nearer and now Fenella, picking up her green skirt, ran down the passage from the Gun-room into the Hall.

She had only just reached it when the horses drew up outside the front door and she stood striving to get her breath, conscious that Lord Corbury who had been running behind her, had stopped too.

"Do not let the Chaise drive away, whatever you do," she whispered, and with a composure she was far from feeling she moved towards the front door.

It was opened to the summer sunshine and even as she reached it a Vision of elegance came up the stone steps.

Madame D'Arbley was dark and extremely alluring. She had eyes that slanted up at the corners and a red mouth which curved invitingly.

She was not beautiful in the accepted sense, but Fenella realised that she had never before in her life seen a woman's face which was so fascinating.

She was dressed in black with touches of white. But her gown was sophisticated, elegant, Parisienne black, which had nothing in common with the sombre, dull mourning assumed by a British widow.

Drawing in a deep breath, Fenella moved forward and dropped a curtsey.

"You must be Madame D'Arbley," she smiled, "I am delighted to welcome you to the Priory."

"*Enchantée, Madame,*" Madame D'Arbley replied. "Has Lord Corbury received my letter?"

She spoke with a pronounced accent which made her words sound extremely attractive.

"Yes, indeed, *Madame,*" Fenella answered. "Will you not come into the Salon?"

She led the way across the Hall, opened the door into the Salon, and invited the French woman to precede her. As she did so she glanced towards the passage and saw that Lord Corbury was waiting there ready to hurry out to the Post Chaise.

Fenella went into the Salon and shut the door quickly.

"Pray be seated, *Madame,*" she said. "I am afraid you have had a long journey. My husband and I were not certain what time you would arrive."

Madame D'Arbley looked surprised. Then she said:

"You have not yet told me your name, *Madame,* although you are aware of mine."

There was only the slightest hesitation before Fenella managed to say:

"I am Lady Corbury, Periquine's . . . w . . . wife!"

"His wife!"

The words were almost a scream and the expression on the French woman's face changed completely. She no longer looked fascinating or attractive. Her slanting eyes narrowed and her curved lips became a straight line.

At that moment it was easy to see that she was not an aristocrat but a petite bourgeoise.

"Married! *C'est impossible! Répétez, s'il vous plaît!* Did you say married?"

"It was of course unlikely you would have heard of it in France," Fenella said in a pleasant conversational tone, "but we did in fact have quite a big wedding, nearly three months ago in London."

"*Mon Dieu!* Are you telling me the truth? My Lord is married to—you?"

"We have known each other for many years," Fenella replied demurely.

The French woman did not speak for a moment, and Fenella realised that she was trembling with rage, but keeping a tight control on herself.

As Fenella was wondering frantically what to say next, Lord Corbury came into the room.

He was smiling and appeared at ease, but Fenella, who knew him so well, was aware that he was in fact nervous and, like all men, apprehensive in case he should become involved in a scene.

At the sight of him, Madame D'Arbley sprang to her feet and moving swiftly towards him placed both her hands in his.

"Periquine, *Mon Cher*, what is this I hear? *C'est incroyable!* How could you do this to me when we have meant so ... much to each other?"

Lord Corbury raised one of her hands to his lips.

"It is delightful to see you, Amaline," he said, "and looking more attractive than ever."

"*Je ne comprends pas!*" Madame D'Arbley said in a voice low and vibrant with emotion. "You promised me marriage, you asked me to share my life with you!"

"I know, my dear," Lord Corbury answered, "but you were not free. I had no idea that your husband would die so soon."

"I told you! I told you that the doctors had not given him long to live!"

"He might however have lingered on for years."

"*Mais il est mort.* How could you be so cruel, so heartless as to forget me so quickly?"

Her voice broke dramatically, and Madame D'Arbley bent her head over Lord Corbury's hand which she now held clasped to her heart.

Lord Corbury gave Fenella a glance which was a wild plea for help.

"I think, Periquine, that you should fetch Madame some refreshment," Fenella said gently. "A glass of Madeira, perhaps? She has been travelling for a long time."

"Yes, yes of course!" Lord Corbury said, disentangling himself from the clinging hands of the French woman.

"Sit down, Amaline, and I will bring you something to drink. That will make you feel better, I am sure of it."

He hurried from the room with the eagerness of a man who was longing to escape from an unpleasant situation.

Madame D'Arbley sat down in an armchair, and drawing a black-edged handkerchief from her satin reticule, applied it to her eyes.

"I cannot believe it is happening to me!" she said. "How I have adored that man! I have been everything to him, his—how do, you say—his slave!"

"I can understand that, Madame," Fenella said sympathetically, "but all men are the same. They feel lonely without a woman to look after them. Perhaps you were too kind and spoilt him so much when he was at your Chateau, that he found life insupportable when you were not beside him."

Fenella hoped such an explanation would salve the pride of the widow. Although Lord Corbury suspected she was interested mainly in his title, Fenella was sure she was also genuinely enamoured of him.

Madame D'Arbley dabbed her eyes and Fenella could not help thinking how attractive she was and how it might even be advantageous for Periquine to marry someone so wealthy.

She could understand his being fascinated by her. It would, she thought, have been impossible for him to avoid having a passionate love affair with such a woman when they were together in France and he had little else to do.

"Do all men," she wondered, "tire so quickly of their loves?"

At one moment they could find some woman irresistible and the next moment wish only to be rid of her. It was a depressing thought, and because Fenella was sorry for Madame D'Arbley, her voice was soft as she said:

"I am sure, *Madame,* you will find real happiness elsewhere. You are young and because you are no longer *une jeune fille,* you are free to do what you like, and you have the money to be able to go anywhere in the world."

"*Nom de Dieu!*" Madame D'Arbley exclaimed, "but I wished to live here—here in this magnificent Château, of which Periquine had talked so often. I saw myself as the Châtelaine, entertaining, being the noble lady of my very handsome, noble husband."

"I think perhaps you would find it very dull living in the country," Fenella answered. "It is different from London, where there are parties, Balls and Assemblies, but here we are very quiet. Some times we go for days without even seeing a neighbour."

"My Lord would be there!" Madame D'Arbley murmured, and that, thought Fenella, was unanswerable as an argument.

Lord Corbury returned, followed by old Barnes carrying a silver salver on which reposed a decanter of Madeira and some wine glasses.

He set it down on a small table and Lord Corbury poured some Madeira into a glass and carried it to Madame D'Arbley.

"I thought it best," he said as he handed her the glass, "to keep your Post Chaise as I know my—er—w . . . Fenella has told you that we have an infectious complaint in the house and I would not wish you, Amaline, to run the risk of catching it."

Fenella noticed how he stumbled and was unable to utter the word, "my wife," and suddenly she felt a little disgusted at the trick they were playing on the French woman, who after all had every reason to believe that Periquine had spoken the truth when he said he loved her.

Aware it would annoy him, at the same time feeling that he deserved to suffer a little for his past behaviour, she rose to her feet.

"I must inquire," she said, "whether the driver of the Post Chaise has been offered a glass of ale."

And before Lord Corbury could think of an excuse to stop her she went from the room.

Outside in the hall she put her hands to her temples. She felt a little ashamed, but at the same time relieved. She might censure him, but at the same time she knew that Periquine would not have been really happy with a French wife who had nothing in common with his interests, his background or the life he enjoyed.

What would Madame D'Arbley know of English sport? Of the demands of a country house and the responsibility of a British nobleman to those who had lived on his estate for generations and whose well-being was as important as his own.

"It would have been an impossible match," Fenella told herself, and yet she could not help feeling sorry for Madame D'Arbley if her heart ached as much as hers did.

How long she stood waiting in the hall she had no idea but it must have been over a quarter of an hour before the door of the Salon opened and Lord Corbury came out with Madame D'Arbley clinging to his arm.

There were tears on her cheeks and he was looking cross and uncomfortable which told Fenella only too clearly what had occurred.

"Oh, there you are, Fenella!" Lord Corbury said in relief. "I have persuaded *Madame* that it is wisest for her to leave at once. Scarlet-fever is a most unpleasant disease, and I would never forgive myself if she were stricken down with it after travelling so many miles to see us."

"Perhaps *Madame*, you will be able to visit us another time," Fenella said.

The French woman did not answer, but still clinging to Corbury's arm proceeded slowly towards the front door.

Only when she looked out and saw the Post Chaise waiting for her outside, did she seem to shiver as if she realised that the happiness with which she had set out on her long journey was finally and completely extinguished.

It was then she turned her face up to Lord Corbury's.

"*Adieu, mon cher,*" she said in a voice that trembled, "I shall never forget you."

She put out her arms as she spoke and putting them round his neck, drew his head down to hers.

She kissed him passionately on the lips and Fenella watching, felt once again the same stabbing pain that she had known when she had watched Periquine kissing the pretty lady in the coach.

This embrace however, did not take so long. Abruptly Madame D'Arbley drew herself free of Lord Corbury and walked down the steps ahead of him.

He helped her into the Post Chaise. Once she was settled she put out her hand and he raised it to his lips.

"I am sorry, Amaline," Fenella heard him say.

Then in a hard sharp tone which seemed almost to ring out, Madame D'Arbley replied:

"Sorry! *Mère de Dieu!* I will never forgive you! Never!"

Lord Corbury stepped back, the driver whipped up his horses and the Post Chaise moved away.

Lord Corbury stood politely on the steps until it was some way down the drive. Then he came back into the Hall. He had taken a handkerchief from his pocket and was mopping his forehead.

"My God!" he ejaculated, "I hope never to go through anything like that again."

He had spoken to Fenella, but when he looked the hall was empty, she was no longer there.

The Dinner-party was an undoubted success. Hetty arrived looking exquisite and completely ravishing, in a gown which only another woman would have known was too elaborate for a quiet evening in the country.

She was also wearing a diamond necklace round her neck and there were diamonds sparkling in the ribbons which were entwined in her fair hair.

She evidently intended to dazzle both Lord Corbury and Sir Nicolas, and Fenella watching her realised she had never known Hetty take so much trouble, or deliberately set out to fascinate.

She was not jealous, what was the use? How could anyone compete with a creature so beautiful, so exquisitely dressed, so sparkling as Hetty?

Fenella had nothing to put on except a plain white muslin she had made herself some months previously to wear in the evening at home.

It was very simple with a fichu veiling her shoulders, her waist encircled with a sash she had worn since she was a child in the Nursery.

Nevertheless, Augustus Baldwyn condescended to ogle her quite outrageously and to be so over-impressive in his compliments that Fenella had the greatest difficulty in not laughing in his face.

More than once she exchanged a glance with Sir Nicolas and remembering their conversation about Augustus saw a twinkle of amusement in his eyes.

The food was unbelievably delicious. Sir Nicolas had certainly spoken the truth when he said that his Valet was an experienced Chef, and even Lord Corbury seemed surprised when course after course was presented to him, each more succulent and exotic than the one before.

"I had no idea that Mrs. Buckle was such a good Cook," Hetty said as she helped herself to a quail in aspic, from a dish skillfully decorated in a manner which would have done credit to Caremé—*le Chef par excellence*, to the Prince Regent.

"She has made a special effort as you are here,"

Lord Corbury replied, and catching Sir Nicolas's eye, Fenella gave a hastily repressed laugh.

"Why do I see so little of you, Fenella, these days?" Augustus Baldwyn asked ingratiatingly.

Fenella wondered if it was the excellent Claret which was making him so mellow.

"I expect because you do not bother to look for me," she answered. "I am either here, or at home, while you, Augustus, I am sure are making your mark amongst the Bucks and Dandies of St. James's."

"You are right, my dear Fenella," he replied conceitedly. "I play my part in the *Beau Monde,* but I would still like to see more of you. I will take you driving in my phaeton one afternoon?"

This, Fenella knew, was a gesture of high condescension from someone as puffed up with his own importance as Augustus Baldwyn.

"How very kind of you," she replied, "but of course I would have to ask Mama if I can drive with a gentleman unchaperoned."

"Good heavens, we do not have to be chaperoned!" Augustus Baldwyn exclaimed. "We have known each other since you were in your cradle, and I am sure your Mother makes no restrictions about your driving with Periquine."

"Periquine is a cousin," Fenella said demurely.

"A distant one," Augustus remarked.

"Periquine's grandmother was my grandmother's first cousin," Fenella said, and glanced at Sir Nicolas as she spoke.

"Of course!" he said quietly, "I realised that was where the Farquhar's were linked with the Corbury family."

"Corbury, or no Corbury," Augustus said in an aggressive voice which showed that he was annoyed at Sir Nicolas joining in the conversation, "I will take you driving, Fenella. You will enjoy it."

There was obviously nothing further to say to this, except to thank him. But Fenella made up her mind that nothing would induce her to go driving with Augustus, if she could possibly avoid it.

Two years ago, when she was only sixteen,
Augustus had called at her home unexpectedly one
afternoon with a box of plants for her Mother from
Lady Baldwyn.

Fenella had been alone when he was announced.
She was sitting in front of the fire drying her hair
which she had just washed.

It rioted like a wave, rich and red over her
shoulders, framing her small face.

"Oh Augustus!" she exclaimed rising to her feet.
"The servants should not have shown you in here!"

"Why not?" he questioned. "You look pretty like
that."

He stood looking down at her, very grown up—
the rich Beau patronising the village maiden! But
there was something about him which made her feel
nervous.

"I will fetch Mama."

"Not so fast," Augustus replied and she saw a
glint of fire in his protruding eyes.

He caught hold of her arm as she would have
passed him to reach the door and Fenella was suddenly afraid.

"Let me go!" she cried.

"When you have given me a kiss!" Augustus
replied thickly in a voice which she felt was slimy
and unpleasant.

"I will do nothing of the sort!" Fenella retorted
trying to pull her arm free of his fat hands.

But he was too strong for her. Inexorably amused
by her struggle to resist him, he drew her into his
arms.

"Let me go! How dare you!"

Fenella was now really frightened, no man had
ever touched her in such a manner. No man had ever
kissed her.

"No! No! I hate you!" she screamed, twisting
and turning but despairingly aware that she could
not escape, could not be free of him.

Then just as with a kind of sick horror she
realised his thick lips were only a few inches from

her own and her voice seemed lost in her throat,
the door opened and her mother entered the room.

Augustus released her and she had collapsed onto
the floor, hiding her frightened face beneath her hair
and feeling somehow defiled because he had touched
her.

"I hate him! I hate him!" she told herself and
was humiliated at her own weakness.

Her feeling had not changed with the passing of
time. She disliked Augustus and every thing he did.

Already she had felt his knee trying to press hers
under the table and he had squeezed her hand in
a meaningful manner when she had greeted him on
arrival.

It had been a mistake, she thought now, to have
chosen a round table for dinner but it was so much
more cosy to sit at the small table in the huge oak-
panelled Banquet Hall than to use the long refectory
which could hold twenty or more people.

Nevertheless it was a gay meal.

Lord Corbury was in good humour because Hetty
was being so charming, and only Fenella realised that
she was deliberately setting out to make Sir Nicolas
jealous by paying more attention to Periquine than
she did to the Premier Baronet.

But she would have been stupid had she not
realised that Sir Nicolas's eyes on the other side of
the table dwelt on her with a sort of kindly expression, and that their secret of knowing who was
providing the dinner seemed to draw them closer than
if they had been mere acquaintances.

It was when the dessert was finished, and the
port and brandy had been taken round deftly by
Sir Nicolas's servants, that Augustus said in his loud
and bumptious manner:

"I congratulate you, Periquine. I did not expect
to enjoy such a good brandy in this house."

"I cannot think why you should be surprised,"
Lord Corbury enquired.

"I understand you were slightly under the hatch,
old boy," Augustus replied. "But this brandy is better

than what I drank last week at Carlton House. I will tell you one thing, if you purchased it in Brighton, I will wager my last sovereign it was smuggled."

"Smuggled!" Fenella ejaculated.

"It is the only way to get good wine nowadays, without paying an exorbitant sum for it," Augustus went on. "And the smugglers know their job! Why a chap was telling me at White's last week that he has made over fifty thousand pounds smuggling in brandy and other luxuries."

"Fifty thousand pounds!"

Fenella heard Lord Corbury slowly repeat the words and felt her heart give a frightening leap.

"No! No!" she wanted to cry, but it was too late.

Lord Corbury was leaning forward across the table, his eyes fixed on Augustus, obviously much impressed.

"I call that extremely interesting, Augustus. Do tell us more."

Augustus was only too willing to oblige. He launched into a long and complicated story of friends who had smuggled in silks, tea and spirits during the war; hidden it in Chapels or under hayricks; conveyed it by ponies to London; and made a fortune on every run.

As she saw Lord Corbury's interest in listening to Augustus's booming voice, Fenella felt the breath being squeezed from her body. She knew as surely as if he had said the words aloud, exactly what plan he was concocting in his mind.

To cause a diversion she suggested to Hetty that they should leave the gentlemen to their drinks. The two girls went upstairs.

"Periquine really gave us a very good dinner," Hetty said condescendingly, "but I cannot think how he could afford all those elaborate dishes."

"He gave the party for you," Fenella said, evading the question.

"It is kind of him," Hetty said in an affected tone regarding her reflection in the mirror and obviously very satisfied with what she saw.

On an impulse, without considering her words, Fenella said:

"Be kind to him, Hetty."

There was a smile of satisfaction at the corners of Hetty's beautiful lips.

"I am kind to him," she replied, "kinder than I have ever been to anyone else."

"He loves you so much," Fenella insisted, "and I would wish him to be happy."

It was true, she thought, that if she could arrange for Hetty to marry Periquine, she would do so because she knew he believed that his happiness lay with her.

"You cannot imagine," Hetty said, "that I could live here in this dreadfully dowdy and uncomfortable house?"

"Not in its present state," Fenella agreed. "But if you really loved Periquine, money would not matter."

Hetty gave an affected little laugh.

"My dear Fenella, you must have been reading some of those rubbishy romances which are written for housemaids. I assure you that money is very essential for happiness. If you imagine that I love Periquine enough to only have one gown, like you, or to sit about in the Priory year after year, without the money to go to London or to travel, then you must be to let in the attic."

"You would be with Periquine," Fenella murmured.

"I like being with Periquine very much," Hetty said, a feline look in her eyes. "But I wonder if I should enjoy it so much if he were my husband? I would see him every day and all day. You know, Fenella, I have always enjoyed variety, especially where men are concerned."

Fenella bit back the words she wanted to say. Instead she said:

"Periquine may inherit some money from his uncle, Colonel Alexander Massingburg-Corbury! He has always hinted Periquine would be his heir."

"When I last saw the Colonel he was leading in the hunting field and took a five-barred gate like a boy of twenty," Hetty replied. "He cannot be many years over fifty and who would want to wait for a deadman's shoes?"

There was no answer to this. Fenella felt she had done her best to further Periquine's suit, but Hetty would not let her heart rule her head.

"Are you going to marry Sir Nicolas?" she asked quietly. "You will hurt Periquine if you do."

"I might," Hetty answered. "I have not really made up my mind."

Even as she spoke Fenella was aware that Sir Nicolas had not yet asked her. But looking at Hetty's beauty, it could only be a question of time.

Fenella could see her own reflection behind Hetty's in the mirror. And she could see her outmoded, old-fashioned, home-made gown, and in front of it the sparkling, radiant Hetty. She was so lovely she was more like a painting than a human-being.

Finding the contrast unbearable, Fenella walked to the other side of the room, and tidied the brushes and combs that she herself had set out on the dressing-table.

"The trouble is," Hetty was saying, in a slow satisfied voice, "I have so many Beaux! I have already had four offers of marriage since the beginning of the year, but Papa's turned them down because he did not think that the gentlemen in question were rich or important enough for me."

She sighed almost ecstatically before she continued.

"Nevertheless, Fenella, I cannot help thinking that however old I grow, there will always be men who will fall in love with me."

"You are very lovely, Hetty," Fenella said with an effort.

"I know," Hetty said. "Did I tell you what His Royal Highness the Prince Regent said the first time he saw me?"

Fenella had heard it about half a dozen times

before, but she appeared attentive, while really she
was thinking of Periquine.

She could not bear that he should break his
heart over Hetty.

Having known her ever since they were children,
she knew that Hetty was both hard and selfish. Although Periquine might be the first man to excite her,
and perhaps had aroused her as no other man had
been able to do, she would never make a sacrifice
of any sort of his sake.

She would never give up one gown, one diamond or even one party to make him happy!

"Perhaps," Fenella thought to herself remembering Madame D'Arbley, "sooner or later I shall have to
save Periquine from Hetty!"

Chapter Six

"IT is like being in a dream," Fenella thought to herself.

The boat was moving smoothly through the water and the only sounds were the creak of the rowlocks and the men's heavy breathing as they bent their backs to the oars.

She could hardly believe it possible that in such a short time Periquine could have arranged everything and they were actually at sea.

Of course it was she who had found the right person for him to contact! Even when she gave him the name she had felt a little tremor of fear in case she was helping him into danger.

But she had known there was no denying his intention to make money by smuggling.

From the moment she had seen his eyes light up at the dining-room table and heard the eagerness in his voice when he asked Augustus to give him more particulars of his friend's smuggling activities, there had been no chance of his turning back.

The idea must have been uppermost in Lord Corbury's mind all through the evening.

As soon as the party from the Hall had departed and Hetty had said her last soft farewell, looking up into his eyes with an expression which no man could resist, the words had seemed to burst from his lips.

"Smuggling! Did you hear what Augustus said, Fenella? That is how we must make some money!"

"It is very dangerous," Fenella said warningly.

"Everything we have done so far is dangerous, but they have still not caught us!" Lord Corbury retorted. "I remember now when I was in London hearing that the traffic of contraband across the Channel since the war ended has never been heavier."

"Exactly," Fenella agreed, "and that was why in January this year, when you were abroad, they appointed a Controller-General of the Preventive Boat Service. His name is Captain Hatchard and he was in the Royal Navy."

"If other people succeed, there is no reason why we should fail," Lord Corbury asserted.

"I heard Papa say that they reckon there are twenty thousand people smuggling contraband goods every year," Fenella replied. "At the same time the Courts and Assizes are filled with those who have been caught and there are more prisoners being transported to Australia than ever before."

"What is the matter with you?" Lord Corbury demanded angrily. "You are always trying to put a damper on me these days!"

"I am not, Periquine, I am not really," Fenella answered. "It is just that I am afraid for . . . you."

She knew as she spoke that it was her love for him that made her fearful. She could not bear to think that he might be in serious trouble with the authorities, or hauled before the Courts for a misdemeanour which could have serious consequences.

"Well, with your help or without your help," Lord Corbury said roughly, "I am going to try my hand at bringing home a cargo. It cannot be so difficult if so many blockheads get away with it!"

Fenella did not answer and after a moment he said:

"And that reminds me—who was waiting on us tonight? I do not remember ever seeing either of those men before."

Fenella hesitated a moment. She wondered if she should tell the truth, knowing it would incense Periquine, but at the same time she never lied to him.

"Sir Nicolas . . . lent us two of his . . . servants," she said after a moment.

"Waringham!" Lord Corbury ejaculated. "But why the devil should he do that? I have no wish to accept his charity!"

He thought for a moment, then added:

"And I imagine it was one of his staff that was doing the cooking. Now I think of it, I cannot believe that Mrs. Buckle was capable of providing the dishes we ate at dinner."

"No, of course she could not," Fenella agreed, "and I assure you that Hetty would not have congratulated you on the food or on the success of the evening if I had not accepted Sir Nicolas's offer of help."

"Are you demented? Do you imagine I wish to be beholden to that stiff neck?" Lord Corbury asked furiously.

"Actually . . . he was not helping . . . you," Fenella said in a low voice.

"Then who was he helping?" Lord Corbury enquired. "I cannot imagine that he wanted my dinner party to be a success, so that I could shine as a host in front of Hetty!"

"He . . . was helping . . . me," Fenella murmured.

"You!"

There was no doubt of the astonishment in Lord Corbury's voice.

"He discovered . . . by chance," Fenella explained uncomfortably, "that I intended to cook the dinner for you. Mrs. Buckle could not do it, and you know as well as I do, Periquine, that old Barnes would never have managed by himself. He can hardly serve two people, let alone five, and he would undoubtedly have got in a terrible tangle with all the different courses."

There was no denying the truth of this and the rage in Lord Corbury's eyes faded a little, but his tone was still truculent as he said:

"Well I think you should have consulted me before accepting Waringham's offer, whatever his motive in making it."

"There was no time to make other arrangements," Fenella pointed out, "and I promise you, Periquine, that I was very worried about the evening from the very moment you told me it had been arranged. And you have to admit that Hetty enjoyed herself and that the food was delicious."

Lord Corbury did not answer for a moment, and she knew he was finding it hard to sustain his anger knowing all too well that what she said was the truth and entirely logical.

Then petulantly he said:

"Well it makes me more convinced than ever than I have to make money—one way or another! Things cannot go on like this, and our ill-gotten gains are certainly not going to last for ever."

He paused a moment, then said:

"Are you going to help me with the smuggling? I am sure you have some local knowledge about people whom I should contact."

"Yes, I will . . . help you" Fenella said with a little sigh.

She knew there was nothing else she could do, and she added almost pleadingly:

"You will take every precaution, Periquine, and not do anything foolhardy? Like you, I do not wish to be transported."

"There is no chance of that," Lord Corbury said sharply. "This is a man's job and you are certainly not coming with me across the Channel."

Fenella laughed.

"Then how, may I ask, are you going to bargain when you reach the other side? I believe it is very important that one should buy cheap to sell dear. Perhaps your French has improved a great deal during the years you were in France, but you were never, with all your cleverness, very proficient at foreign languages."

Lord Corbury grinned.

"I am told I am a most convincing gapster when it comes to making love."

"That of course is very helpful!" Fenella said

sarcastically. "Unless you are buying the brandy from a female which is not likely! Either I come with you, Periquine, or I will not tell you whom to contact in the first place. And if you go floundering around asking the wrong people, there is every likelihood of your making the authorities suspicious before you start."

"All right, all right!" Lord Corbury agreed. "Do not nag me! Trust a woman always to get—her own way! Tell me where I should go and whom I should see."

Fenella had heard for some years of a Mr. Renshaw who lived in Hellingly and who was a by-word amongst the local villagers.

"I'll wager this must be some of Renshaw's spirit," they would say in the local Inn, if the rum or brandy was of good quality.

And when a man smelt pleasantly of a good tobacco, there was always someone who would clap him on the back and ask if he had been "seeing Renshaw" lately.

Lord Corbury rode off to Hellingly the next day, and Fenella for once agreed it would be unwise for her to accompany him. He came back elated as a school-boy.

"Renshaw is a splendid chap!" he told Fenella. "He understood exactly what I wanted almost before I had to ask his help. He says there is a boat that I can buy and it is a first class bargain. It is very light, very fast and has not done more than half a dozen trips."

"Then why is it being sold?" Fenella asked.

For a moment Lord Corbury looked embarrassed. Then he said:

"The crew had a bit of bad luck. They ran straight into a Revenue Cutter."

He saw Fenella's expression and added quickly:

"Renshaw says it is a thing that might happen once in a million times. As a matter of fact he suspects they had all been drinking, a thing which never happens if there is someone of authority in command.

Obviously it is important to cross as quickly as possible—not much over three hours on a smooth sea—pick up the cargo and get home before dawn."

"The nights are not long this time of year," Fenella objected. "I have always understood that despite the rough seas it is better to go in October or November."

"I am not going to wait until then," Lord Corbury said positively. "As a matter of fact I put that very point to Renshaw and he told me there is a summer morning mist over the Channel which is just as effective as a November fog."

It was impossible to quench his enthusiasm, and soon Fenella found herself carried away with the excitement of it all and was prepared to listen to the details which Lord Corbury had culled from Mr. Renshaw.

"Renshaw was telling me that last night," he related, "a boat with which he was concerned with a crew of 26 brought back a ton of leaf tobacco in bales of 60 lbs, fifty half-ankers of brandy and gin and thirty chests of tea, to the value of £10,000."

"But surely you are not having so large a crew?" Fenella exclaimed.

"No, this boat that I bought from him is only built for ten," Lord Corbury answered. "At the same time Renshaw thinks that with skilful buying—and you were right there, Fenella, to buy right is essential —we could make five to seven thousand pounds profit a trip."

"It is a lot!" Fenella exclaimed.

"What is more," Lord Corbury went on, "a golden guinea will fetch 27 shillings in England now and much more on the other side of the Channel. That gold in the Priest's Hole is worth a great deal more than we thought!"

"How much will you have to pay the crew?" Fenella asked.

"Renshaw says that if I employ them regularly they should get £1 a week each as wages, and £10 for every successful run."

"And you actually bought the boat?" Fenella enquired.

"Of course I have," Lord Corbury replied. "I am not such a fool as to let such a bargain slip through my fingers. And Renshaw is arranging everything for me—the boat, the men and the ponies who will take away the cargo immediately on our return."

"What does he ask for himself?"

"Seventeen per cent of the cargo and my word of honour that if we are caught his name will never be mentioned."

"I suppose he is trustworthy," Fenella said doubtfully. "After all he has everything to gain and nothing to lose! I expect you will have to pay cash for the boat immediately."

"My dear girl, Renshaw is a business man," Lord Corbury said. "I promised to take the money over to him tomorrow, with of course payment in advance for the ponies and the men who will carry the cargo to London on our return."

"It all sounds so easy," Fenella thought at the time.

Even now in the darkness of the night and feeling of the boat moving under her, she could hardly credit they were actually embarked on such a wild adventure.

Once again she was dressed in the clothes that Periquine had worn at Eton and which she had worn when they had visited Isaac Goldstein's house. Even Lord Corbury had thought this a wise precaution.

"I shall tell the men you are my young brother," he said. "There is a superstition about it being unlucky for a ship to carry a woman at sea and I am certain they would not want to take one on a journey where they were risking their lives."

"Yes, I think it is sensible to say I am a boy," Fenella agreed.

"And do not speak if you can help it," Lord Corbury admonished her, "or your voice will give you away."

They had been forced to leave the Priory in day-

light and Fenella had been half afraid that someone would see her riding astride before they were
out of the immediate vicinity of her home.

But fortunately by riding in the shelter of the
woods and through the fields, they had escaped notice
and reached Hellingly just as the sun was sinking.

Lord Corbury rode without pausing through the
little hamlet with its Inn and small grey stone church,
and they continued across the Downs until they
reached the small creek where the men were to be
waiting for them.

For a moment Fenella seeing no-one thought
their plan had failed and Lord Corbury would be
disappointed. But almost like magic men appeared
from behind rocks and from some caves low down
at sea level.

The boat had been covered with fisherman's nets
and hidden so effectively that anyone passing would
hardly have given it a second glance.

By the time the nets had been removed and
Lord Corbury had inspected the boat, the dusk was
falling and it was time to go.

The oarsmen who were tough, sturdy yokels with
strong muscles, carried stout ashpoles six feet in
length which was known as bats. It was these weapons which were very effective in a fight which had
earned them the name of batmen by which they
were known to the Revenue Officers.

There was very little talking and every man
seemed to know what was expected of him.

In the shortest possible time the boat was carried down to the edge of the water and Lord Corbury
made a gesture to Fenella to come forward and seat
herself in the bow.

He himself would obviously sit in the stern with
his hand on the tiller, and Fenella would have wished
to be beside him. But she knew it was not the moment to argue.

Accordingly she did as she was told and realised,
as she sat down on some coiled ropes and watched

the men taking their places at the oars, that the boat was very light.

There was plenty of room for the cargo, but she knew that it inevitably would slow down the speed of their return journey and make it more dangerous.

What was more, she told herself, the Preventive boats would wish to catch the smugglers red-handed and would therefore patrol the English Coast waiting for those who broke the law to return laden with their contraband from France.

Though there was no point now in dwelling on the dangers of what they were doing, Fenella could not help being apprehensive, and she wondered if Hetty had any idea how much Periquine was prepared to risk for her sake.

"Whatever happens we are together," she thought to herself and knew she could not have borne to be left behind wondering what was happening and knowing that Periquine was risking his life.

"I love him," she whispered to herself and wondered if he would ever realise how much he meant to her.

"Perhaps if we were both condemned to die, I could tell him," she thought.

Then she shuddered at the idea. How could Periquine, so handsome, so full of life, die? And for something so relatively unimportant as money!

It was a warm evening with very little wind and the men were making good progress.

An hour went by and another passed without incident, and then almost before Fenella expected it there was the dark shadow ahead of the French coast, and Lord Corbury was giving low voiced orders to the men to ship their oars.

Still without speaking, two men jumped overboard and dragged the boat up onto the shingle, and then they were all stepping out into the softly lapping waves.

As Fenella rose a little uncertainly to her feet, Lord Corbury lifted her in his arms and carried her

a little way up the beach so that she did not get her
feet wet.

"I am sure this is the place," he whispered.
"Renshaw described it to me exactly."

They walked on and after they had gone only a
few yards a man appeared out of the darkness.

"*Rouge et noir*," Lord Corbury said, giving the
password in what Fenella thought privately was un-
mistakably a British accent.

In reply the man brought from under the dark
cloak he was wearing a lantern which he held for a
moment so that he could see Lord Corbury's face.

He was appearently satisfied because he turned
on his heel and with an abrupt *Suivez-moi* walked
ahead.

They followed him and in a very short while
found themselves in a shed which was built on the
edge of the beach. Fenella realised it was nothing
more or less than a roughly constructed warehouse.

Here there were hundreds of tubs of brandy and
gin, bales of tobacco and tea, rolls of silks, in fact
every sort of ware that it was possible to imagine,
and all ready for sale so long as the Frenchmen
could get their hands on the English gold they so
greedily coveted.

The men with whom they were dealing were
sharp-faced and hard-eyed. At first Fenella merely
translated what they said to Lord Corbury, and then
repeated his answers back to them in French.

But soon she found herself in the midst of the
argument being unable to resist the cut and thrust of
what was undoubtedly a duel of wits.

It was when finally they had agreed a figure for
the brandy and tobacco which Lord Corbury had decided were the only goods he would purchase on this
trip, that one of the Frenchmen said admiringly:

"Your young brother, *Monsieur*, drives a hard
bargain! He is so sharp that he might be a woman.
He has left us precious little profit on this deal, I can
promise you."

Lord Corbury understood the gist of this and replied quickly:

"There will be other trips—I might even buy a bigger boat. It just depends how successful I am the first time."

"You will have no difficulty in disposing of these, *Monsieur*," the Frenchman answered. "Your brother has beguiled out of us the best brandy and the very best tobacco. There is many that would cheat you, but not us."

"I hope not," Lord Corbury said dryly.

Then one of the Frenchmen ran off to fetch the crew who carried the cargo down to the ship.

Lord Corbury paid over the gold which he carried in a leather bag round his waist. Each oarsman, Fenella had noticed, had a long leather purse slung to his belt. And in this they had stored the guinea with which Lord Corbury had paid them before they started their journey.

Then quietly without wasting time in goodbyes or even the expressions of good will usually so prevalent in French conversation, they set off for home.

This, Fenella knew, was where the danger really lay, and yet everything seemed so quiet and peaceful. They had not encountered a single ship or boat on their outward journey, and it appeared as if their luck would hold and the homeward run would be just as uneventful.

The sky was overcast and it seemed as if there was a promise of rain. Fenella knew that would be in their favour, though it would be uncomfortable for the crew.

The men were rowing well. They had started off on leaving a little unevenly, but now the boat was being so skilfully handled that it seemed to shoot through the water with every stroke.

It was not very comfortable sitting in the bow now that it was filled with barrels and bales. Fenella had no room for her legs as she had had on the outward journey, and the smell of tobacco was so strong that it made her eyes sting.

She was however growing apprehensive because, although they were still in mid Channel, it seemed to her that the sky was lightening perceptibly.

She longed to ask Periquine if he was worried too, but he was right at the other end of the boat and between them were the sweating oarsmen, their breathing sounding quite noisy in the stillness all around them.

Then, with a relief which made Fenella realise how much the tension had been growing inside her, they ran into a sea mist.

It was not very dense, but there was enough for her to feel that if afforded a little cover; for there was no doubt that now the night-sky was paling and there was a faint promise of dawn in the east.

On and on they went, on and on, until Fenella felt her eyelids dropping and knew that the tobacco was having a narcotic effect on her.

She was indeed almost asleep when suddenly there was the sound of voices.

She sat up quickly with a jerk. The sound came from their right and she realised immediately it was from another ship.

Lord Corbury had heard it too and he said quietly.

"Lift your oars."

The men obyed him taking their oars out of the water. But it was too late! If they had heard another ship approaching, the ship had also heard them.

"Who are you?" a voice shouted across the water. "Heave to in the name of the King!"

It was a Revenue Cutter and Fenella almost screamed the words aloud. Then she heard Lord Corbury say, still in a low voice but with an unmistakable note of command:

"Row—we will run for it!"

The men put their oars back in the sea.

"Steady," Lord Corbury said, still in a voice that only his crew could hear, "take your timing from me."

There was just one moment of panic and then the men's combined effort seemed almost to lift the boat out of the water.

"Heave to or I shoot!" the voice called.

It was now behind them and slightly further away than it had been before.

As the men pulled with what appeared to be almost super human strength, there was the sudden explosion and the sound of a bullet whizzing above them.

"Keep your heads down," Lord Corbury said sharply.

The mist was all around them but it was growing lighter and Fenella strained her eyes forward in hope of seeing the cliffs ahead.

Then came another explosion and yet another, and she suddenly felt something sear her arm like a red-hot iron.

She gave a little cry and slipped back against the bales, but no-one heard her because at that moment Lord Corbury was saying triumphantly:

"We are nearly out of range! A few more strokes and they will not catch us on this trip!"

The Revenue Cutter fired again. Lord Corbury was right. The report was some way behind them. Fenella sat very still her hand on her arm.

For a moment she felt desperately faint, and then she realised that the bullet cutting its way through the thick cloth of her jacket had only seared the fleshy part of her arm.

She was wise enough to realise it was not a serious wound, but at the same time it was extremely painful.

"I am feeling the effects of the shock," she told herself sensibly, "and there is no point in making a fuss or drawing attention to what has happened until we are on shore. We have escaped one Revenue Cutter, but there may be others."

She could feel the blood on her fingers, but her heart was beginning to beat normally again and she no longer felt faint.

Now she began to wonder how she could explain away such a wound to her mother and whether it would be better to seek out a doctor and have it bandaged before she returned home.

She was still wondering what would be best when she realised the boat was running into Hellingly Creek and the men were springing out to pull it up from the water.

Lord Corbury walked quietly up the beach looking for the ponies that should have been waiting for them, but instead there was only a small boy who crept up to him out of the shadows.

"'Tis th' military Guv! Oi'was to tell ye there be soldiers all along th' cliff," he whispered. "They told Oi' to say tis best to sink th' boat and th' cargo in th' creek. T'aint safe to do nowt else."

"Damn it! Is that the truth?" Lord Corbury enquired fiercely.

"That's wat Oi' were a'told to tell ye, Guv," the boy said and disappeared.

Lord Corbury went back to the men who were waiting.

"There is trouble," he said. "They suggest we sink the boat in the creek, but that would ruin the tobacco although the brandy will be all right. Shall we put the bales in the caves?"

"Aye, we'll do that," one of the men replied.

They seized the bales from around Fenella and hurriedly carried them into the caves.

Feeling shaken and rather limp, Fenella moved out of their way noting that Lord Corbury was busy counting out the sovereigns for the crew and handing them to their leader.

"Sink the boat," he ordered, "and disappear!"

The cork was pulled from the bung-hole and the boat sank quickly just inside the creek.

By now it was light enough to see it disappearing under the surface, and Fenella wondered despairingly if all their efforts had been in vain. But there was little time for introspection.

The men had taken their wage and were van-

ishing into the mist which still hung over the creek
but was becoming more transparent every moment.
Now another man appeared leading their horses.

"Ye'd be wise t' get away quick like. There be
soldiers everywhere!"

"Thank you," Lord Corbury said and rewarded
him with a guinea.

He swung himself into the saddle.

"Will you . . . help me?" Fenella asked. "I am
. . . afraid I have . . . hurt my arm."

Lord Corbury noticed her for the first time. In
the brightening light it was easy to see the blood on
her fingers and on the arm of her jacket.

"What has happened?" he asked dismounting.

"One of the bullets grazed me."

"Good God, why did you not say so!" he exclaimed.

"I am all right. Just put me in the saddle, it is
difficult to mount with only one hand."

"We will have it attended to as soon as we are
out of this mess," he said harshly as he lifted her
onto her horse.

Fortunately the wound was in Fenella's left arm
and she picked up the reins with her right hand.

"I can ride," she said.

Lord Corbury remounted.

"I wonder which would be the best way to . . ."
he was saying when they both heard the sound of
approaching hooves.

"Quick!" Lord Corbury cried and turning his
horse he rode away in the opposite direction followed
by Fenella.

They had only gone a very short distance before they realised they were being followed. There
was no doubt that horses were being urged after
them and that men were shouting instructions to
each other.

Lord Corbury spurred his horse.

"We must not be caught, not with your arm in
that state, there would be too much explaining to do."

Fenella realised too how incriminating it would

be for her to be found wounded and wearing boy's clothes, with no reasonable explanation for their being near Hellingly Creek.

Fortunately both the horses were fresh. They had been stabled while Lord Corbury and Fenella had crossed the Channel.

At the same time the mist was clearing and as soon as they were clear of Hellingly Village and setting off across some flat land, Fenella looked back over her shoulders and saw they were being pursued by four soldiers.

There was no mistaking the red coats of the Dragoon Guards and she knew that without questioning Periquine that he had seen them too.

The soldiers were well mounted and Fenella and Lord Corbury had only a short start. Their one advantage was that both of them knew the country well.

They had ridden over this land so often that it was as familiar to them as their own Parks, but it was also open country and they were well in sight of their pursuers and spurring their horses who seemed to realise that an extra effort was required of them.

"Are you all right?" Lord Corbury managed to shout as they thundered over a field of clover and heedless of the damage galloped on over a field of young wheat.

"Yes, I am all right!" Fenella answered.

She was thankful she was riding astride and could grip the saddle with her knees. Her horse kept beside Lord Corbury's without her having to guide it and both animals knew instinctively they were heading for home.

They galloped on and on. Now the Priory was not far ahead but, though the soldiers behind had not gained any distance on them, it was still impossible to lose them.

"Where shall we go?" Lord Corbury asked, the words coming almost gaspingly between his lips.

For a moment Fenella did not answer. To go to their own stables, she thought, would be dis-

astrous, since the soldiers would follow them there.
To try and hide in the woods . . . The answer came
to her in a flash.

"The Church-in-the-Woods!" she shouted. "The
Crypt!"

She saw Lord Corbury grin at her and then they
were thundering through thick trees which encircled
the back of the Priory, twisting their way through
the heavy trunks to where the Monk's Chapel which
had been left derelict for years had been restored
for the old Vicar.

Surrounded by trees, the Chapel was difficult to
find unless one knew the way, and as Lord Corbury
and Fenella drew their sweating horses to a standstill in front of it, they realised that for the first time
they had an advantage over the soldiers.

They could hear them in the distance, but they
were not as near as they had been.

"Get the Crypt open," Lord Corbury said sharply.
"I will manage the saddles."

He pulled the bridle and saddle from his own
horse as he spoke, and gave him a slap which sent
him careering off through the wood towards home,
and as Fenella ran into the Church he turned towards
her horse.

The Crypt of the Church-in-the-Woods was where
the monks had buried many of their brothers.

Periquine and Fenella had found it when they
were children and had often hidden there from tutors
and governesses, well aware that few people knew
of what was, from a child's point of view, the perfect
secret place.

The Crypt door was a stone slab which lying
flat on the floor of the Church was almost indiscerni-
ble to those who had no knowledge of its existence.

There was a special way to open it, and it had
been constructed by stone-masons who knew that the
profane must not be allowed to enter what to the
monks was a holy place.

Inside the little Church there was a smell of
age, dust and decay which Fenella had known all

her life and loved because it was so much a part of her childhood.

As she entered the Church there was a scuttle of tiny animals running under the oak pews and the flutter of wings from birds which were perched in the rafters.

Fenella slipped the catch and pulled up the big stone finding it difficult with one hand, and almost as she did so Periquine came staggering in through the door carrying the two saddles.

He flung them down the aperture, and without waiting for him to speak Fenella slipped down the steep staircase and he followed her, closing the heavy stone door behind him.

It was completely dark and very cold in the Crypt, but Fenella with a sigh of relief knew that they were safe. She put out her foot tentatively so as not to stumble over the saddles and then as Lord Corbury came down the steps to stand beside her, they heard the soldiers arrive outside the Church.

Fenella slipped her hand into Periquine's. Her fingers were trembling and he gripped them tightly. She was frightened but Periquine was there, and she thought wildly that nothing mattered except that they were together.

"There's be a Church 'ere, Sir," they heard a man say.

"Then that is where they will be hiding. Get inside and be sure there is not another door through which they can escape."

The voice was that of an Officer, cultured and authoritative. A moment later there was the clump of heavy boots on the flagged floor above them.

The first soldier was obviously joined by the Officer and two other men.

"They dinna seem te be 'ere, Sir."

"Run your sword under the pews," the Officer commanded, "and look behind the altar."

"If us finds 'em here, Sir," another man remarked, "they be a takin' sanctuary, we canna touch 'em."

"I will touch smugglers wherever I find them!"

the Officer answered grimly. "Go on, you fools, they must be here. I saw the marks of their horses' hooves outside."

"They must 'ave gone on, Sir, they ain't 'ere."

"Two of you ride on through the wood," the Officer said.

Fenella heard the men ride off. She wanted to ask Periquine if he thought the fact that the horses were hot and sweating would prove incriminating. Then she answered the question herself.

By now both the horses would have headed for their own stables. It was not likely that anyone seeing a horse moving saddleless across a field would think there was anything unusual about it. It had been clever of Periquine, she thought, to remove the saddles.

Above them there came the Officer's voice.

"They must be somewhere! Two men cannot vanish as quickly as that!"

"I'll swear they're not 'ere, Sir. They must be 'iding in th' bushes somewhere."

"Then look for them, you dolt!" the Officer said sharply.

There was no mistaking the disappointment and anger in his voice. He had thought to make a capture, which would have been a feather in his cap. But his victims had eluded him.

"There be nowhere else t' search, Sir."

"Very well, we had better go back to Hellingly and see what we can find out locally. There is no doubt that a boat was expected and that these two men had something to do with it. We have lost them, blast it! They should give us better mounts in the Army! If they want us to catch smugglers, they must afford the best horse-flesh."

The Officer's angry voice seemed to echo round the walls of the little Church. Then they heard him stamp noisily down the steps and a moment later there was a jingle of bridles and the sound of hooves moving away.

It was then Fenella gave a deep sigh which

seemed to come from the very depths of her being.

She realised now that she had been holding her breath and had been rigid with fear all the time the soldiers were searching for them overhead.

"We have done it!" she heard Lord Corbury exclaim. "We have escaped once again, Fenella, and by God this time it really was by the skin of our teeth!"

He let go of her hand to put his arm round her waist and drew her towards him in one of the affectionate hugs that he gave her so often. And in the darkness he bent his head to kiss her cheek.

Without realising it Fenella had raised her face towards his. Her lips were smiling a little because she too knew they had escaped captivity only by a hair's breath.

Then instead of kissing Fenella's cheek as he had intended, Lord Corbury's lips found hers.

Just for one second she was still with surprise at his touch, until as if it were a streak of lightning, a feeling of wonder and rapture struck through her whole body.

It was impossible to move, impossible to do anything but know that her lips were soft yet captive beneath his and his kiss evoked within her a wonder such as she had never known existed.

A gleam of fire flickered into life and she felt it burning through her until it reached her lips.

The pressure of Periquine's mouth on hers deepened. Instinctively he put out his other hand to draw her closer and gripped her arm.

The agony of the pain was worse than when the bullet had seared its way through her flesh. Fenella gave a little gasp and the darkness seemed to close in upon her. . . .

Chapter Seven

THE old maid put a rug over Fenella's knees and arranged a pillow behind her head in an easy-chair set under the shade of a big lime tree.

"Now just you rest, Miss Fenella," she said firmly, "and no running over to the Priory when my back is turned to go afussing over Master Periquine. He can look after himself for a while and it'll do him good."

"Did he seem all right when he came here yesterday, Anna?" Fenella asked.

"There was nothing wrong with—him," Anna answered sharply.

She had been in the service of Fenella's mother and father for over thirty years and had looked after Fenella, loved her and scolded her since she was a small child.

It was always Anna who saved her from the worst consequences of her escapades with Periquine, who mitigated the punishment of being sent to bed early by creeping up the back stairs with milk and biscuits without her mother's knowledge.

It was to Anna that Lord Corbury had carried Fenella the night after the smuggling expedition, and Fenella had heard at least a hundred times what a shock it had been.

"Coming here at the crack of dawn with you as white as a sheet and Master Periquine not much better!

" 'She's been shot in the arm, Anna!' he says to me.

" 'And who's done that I'd like to know?' " I enquired, not that I really had to ask the question!

" 'It's not the first time I've spoken to you, Master Periquine, about playing around with dangerous firearms,' I says to him."

"You must not be too hard on him, Anna," Fenella pleaded again and again.

"Hard on him!" old Anna gave a snort. "It's time someone spoke their mind to Master Periquine and tells him to behave himself. You'd have thought the Army would have given him a sense of responsibility. But there are some who never give up playing around like a mischievous small boy however old they get!"

Fenella could not help laughing.

It was true that Anna was the one person who would speak her mind whatever the circumstances, and she was quite sure that while she was unconscious Anna in our own words had let Periquine "have it!"

But in fact it was not surprising that both Periquine and Anna had been worried about her. She had run a high temperature the next morning, but on her insistence Anna had not sent for the doctor.

"You must tell Mama I injured myself by a fall when out riding," she said, "and I do not want a physician. You know as well as I do, Anna, that you can nurse me better than anyone else."

The flattery had its intended effect.

Anna produced her own special potions which brought down the temperature, and the next two days the wound on Fenella's arm was healing and she was no longer feverish.

At the same time she felt rather weak, and now she was up and dressed she was glad to sit quietly under the trees and know that she was being looked after, even though Anna invariably showed her love by bullying her.

"I'll bring you a glass of milk in half an hour's time," Anna was saying, "and you'll drink every drop of it if I have to stand over you to make you do it."

"I do not like milk, Anna," Fenella said petulantly.

"It'll do you good," Anna retorted, and Fenella knew that she would have to drink it.

She watched the old maid walking back across the lawn towards the house with a warm look of affection in her eyes.

She wondered how many punishments in the past she and Periquine had avoided by Anna protecting them from the wrath of their parents.

She was thankful that, after she had fainted in his arms in the darkness of the crypt, Periquine had had the sense to take her up the back-stairs to her room and to fetch Anna.

As Fenella thought of the crypt, a little thrill went through her as she remembered what she had felt when Periquine's lips had found hers after the soldiers had left.

She had only to think of it to feel again that strange rapture which was unlike anything she had ever imagined she could feel.

She had always thought it would be wonderful to be kissed by Periquine, but she did not realise that the thrill of it would sear its way through her body, or that she would feel as if a sudden flame awoke something within herself so fierce, so passionate that she was almost afraid of its strength.

"It was wonderful!" she whispered to herself, and then questioned whether it had meant anything to Periquine.

Had he too felt that strange magnetism which had held their lips spellbound so that neither of them could move? Had he also known the magic which had made her completely his captive, so that she felt she was surrendering to him not only her lips, but her heart and her soul?

Then like a bitter blow she remembered that Periquine was in love with Hetty.

What she was feeling now must be the emotion which he felt when, with that exquisite pink and white face raised to his, he kissed those perfect rose-bud lips.

"How can I be so foolish as to imagine for one moment that I could mean anything to him!" Fenella thought. "How can there be any comparison between Hetty and myself?"

She knew only too well what she looked like with her worn-out faded dresses, the freckles powdering her small nose, her dark-red hair riotiously over her head, instead of being elegantly arranged by a fashionable hairdresser.

"Stop being so idiotic!" she told herself severely. "You are just Periquine's cousin, a girl for whom he has a warm affection but whom he regards as nothing but a romp. A child he has known all his life, for whom he has the same sort of love as he would give to his sister."

Because she felt so weak the tears came into her eyes at the thought of how far removed he was from her in spirit, however close they might be in reality.

"Tomorrow I will go to the Priory," Fenella told herself, "Periquine's bed-room will be in a nice mess by now and I am sure old Barnes will have forgotten to press his cravats, Mrs. Buckle will have cooked him the same dish over and over again, because she always forgets what she has served the day before."

She was planning how she would get up early and would ride over before Periquine had time to leave the house.

He had taken to going first thing to see the farms that were being repaired, and she also had a suspicion that either today or tomorrow he would go back to Hellingly to see what had happened to the cargo.

It would not have been wise to go before.

The military would still be making searching investigations along that part of the coast, perhaps questioning Mr. Renshaw and anyone else they could find in the village.

They would learn nothing, Fenella was sure of that, because the villagers of Hellingly had been involved in smuggling activities all through the war and were far too careful of themselves to turn informer.

There were horrifying tales about the brutality of smugglers to those who denounced them to the authorities or even to those who had been bullied into disclosing the whereabouts of a hidden cargo.

Fenella was sure that all who lived in the Hellingly district would be far more frightened of Mr. Renshaw and the smugglers than of the soldiers.

At the same time it would be dangerous for Periquine to be seen there, and she only hoped he had been sensible enough to keep away.

Anna had told her that he had called to enquire how she was both yesterday and the day before. But her mother would not permit him to come up to her bed-room.

This was a somewhat belated effort of propriety on the part of Mrs. Lambert, but it made Fenella realise that at least the fact that she was grown up had percolated into her parent's mind.

"I want to see Lord Corbury, Anna," she had said to the old maid.

"I'm not bringing him up the back-stairs without your mother's knowledge," Anna had declared. "He's done enough damage to you already, without getting you into any more trouble."

"I have some very important matters to discuss with him," Fenella pleaded.

"Then they'll have to wait!" Anna said with a determination in her voice which Fenella knew was final.

"Today I shall be able to see him," Fenella told herself and felt he was sure to call.

Then despondently she thought that perhaps he was not missing her company and would be too engaged on other matters to make enquiries about her health for the third time.

"He will not be pleased," she thought miserably, "that his plans have gone awry."

At the same time, once the soldiers had moved

away, they could salvage the boat and Mr. Renshaw would arrange for the brandy and tobacco to be fetched by the ponies.

The thought was cheering, and then almost like a cold hand clutching at her heart, Fenella remembered that this would not be the end of Periquine's smuggling activities.

If he received even more than £5,000 for this cargo, it would still not be enough.

They would have to go to France again and yet again, and at the thought of the dangers of such journeys Fenella felt almost faint.

It seemed to her inevitable that sooner or later they must be caught.

T' odds were against them. How ever could they slip through the mesh every time with preventive boats and soldiers waiting at every creek all along the coast and being permanently on the alert!

"I cannot bear it; I cannot," she whispered to herself.

She shut her eyes against the thought of being rowed backwards and forwards across the Channel expecting every moment to hear a voice coming to them out of the mist commanding them to "Heave to."

Then as they dashed for safety the bullets whizzing over their heads! Perhaps the next time one would strike Periquine rather than herself!

Her eyes were closed, but Fenella was suddenly aware of someone standing beside her chair.

She looked up, hoping it was Periquine, and saw Sir Nicolas looking down at her. A faint smile came to her lips, but before she could speak he said harshly:

"Your maid tells me you have been wounded in the arm. What has that young jackanapes done to you now?"

There was so much anger in his tone that Fenella looked at him in surprise.

"Anna should have told you nothing of the sort," she said weakly, "it is a secret."

"Then it should not be one," Sir Nicolas snapped. "Corbury should be told to behave himself. I always thought he was irresponsible, but I imagined he was sportsman enough to be able to carry a gun without injuring anyone—least of all you!"

"You must not blame Periquine!" Fenella said hastily.

"I do blame him!" Sir Nicolas retorted. "And I intend to tell him what I think of him. It is time someone put an end to his rampaging about like a wild bull."

Fenella would have smiled at his words had she not been worried that he was blaming Periquine unjustly.

"It is not what you . . . think," she said. "Please do not be . . . angry with Periquine."

"Angry? I am completely disgusted by his behaviour! How could he have shot you? What was he doing out with a gun at this time of year?"

There was so much suspicion in Sir Nicolas's voice that Fenella found herself saying weakly:

"It was not . . . Periquine who . . . wounded me."

"Then who was it?" Sir Nicolas required.

"A Revenue Officer."

"Good God!"

Sir Nicolas ejaculated the words, then sat down on a hard chair as if his legs could no longer support him.

He was exquisitely dressed as usual, the points of his collar beneath his white cravat high above his chin, his coat fitting superbly over his shoulders.

His fob glittered in the sunlight against the pale yellow of his skin-tight pantaloons, and the high polish on his Hessian boots made Fenella long to bring Periquine's boots up to the same pitch of perfection.

"What did you say?" Sir Nicolas managed to gasp after a moment's pause.

Fenella gave a little laugh.

"I am trusting you with our lives, since I somehow believe that you are a friend."

"You mean that you were smuggling?" Sir Nicolas asked, the words coming almost in a strangled manner from in between his lips.

Fenella nodded.

"We had brought a cargo back safely across the Channel," she explained, "but when we reached the creek from which we had set out, we had to sink the boat. The soldiers were looking for us and Periquine and I only escaped by a miracle."

"Corbury must be demented!" Sir Nicolas exclaimed.

There was so much horror in his voice that Fenella could not help laughing.

"I thought I had to tell you, Sir Nicolas, not only to excuse Periquine, but because I knew how shocked you would be," she smiled, "but all is well. The bullet from the Preventive Ship only just grazed my arm. But naturally I could not tell Mama what had happened."

"If you did, perhaps she would have the good sense to hand that young fool over to the authorities," Sir Nicolas said grimly.

"Do not forget that, if Periquine is transported, I shall have to go with him," Fenella said provocatively. "That is why I am quite sure, Sir Nicolas, you will not betray our secret."

"I have a mind to give Corbury a good thrashing," Sir Nicolas said, "which is what he deserves!"

Fenella laughed again.

Sir Nicolas was a tall up-standing man, but Periquine was taller and certainly broader of shoulder. She was quite certain who would be the winner if it came to a trial of strength.

"We were not caught and my wound is better already," she said consolingly. "In two or three days there will be only a mark on my arm to show what happened."

"How could you risk your life in such a foolish manner?" Sir Nicolas asked.

There was a different note in his voice now, and Fenella's eyes fell before his as she said:

"I had to go. Periquine could never have managed the bargaining without me."

"I forbid you to do this again!" Sir Nicolas said. "Do you hear me, Fenella, I absolutely forbid you!"

Fenella's eyes opened in surprise and as she looked at him enquiringly, he said:

"You need someone to look after you, Fenella. Will you marry me?"

"Sir Nicolas!"

There was no doubt that Fenella was astonished.

"I never . . . thought," she murmured, "I never . . . dreamt . . ."

She stopped and said quickly:

"But you want to marry Hetty."

"I never really wanted to marry her," Sir Nicolas replied. "I considered the idea because she is so beautiful and I thought that she would look well in the family diamonds. But that was before I met you."

"But I am the last person you could possibly want as a wife," Fenella protested. "You know that I say just what comes into my head. I have not an air of consequence or any of the attributes that you think so important."

"I did think them important." Sir Nicolas answered, "but since I have known you, Fenella. I have realised that all my values were wrong."

He leant forward as he spoke and took her hand in his.

"It was meeting you," he said quietly, "that showed me how much I am missing in life."

"What are you missing?" Fenella asked curiously.

"Laughter, gaiety, a joy of living such as you have and which I have never found in anyone else," he replied. "Perhaps I have never known that it existed. You see, I realise now, Fenella, that I have been brought up in a golden cage."

"Too much money?" Fenella said softly.

"And not enough love," Sir Nicolas went on. "My mother died when I was very young and my father was determined I should be worthy to succeed to his position when he was no longer there. He was obsessed by the importance of our family."

Sir Nicolas drew a deep breath.

"I know now how lonely and perhaps in many ways unhappy my childhood was. I was not allowed to go to school."

"Why not?" Fenella enquired.

"My father wished to supervise my education himself. I had a succession of tutors until I went to Oxford."

"Were you not happy there?" Fenella enquired.

"By that time I can see now quite clearly I had become a pompous bore," Sir Nicolas said frankly. "I suppose in some ways my attitude was due to shyness and the fact that I had never been allowed to associate with boys of my own age. I was proud to the point of absurdity and naturally in consequence I made few friends."

"I can understand what you must have felt," Fenella said, "but how could your father have been so cruel as not to allow you the ordinary interests and happiness that a child finds with other children of his own age?"

"Looking back as I have been doing these past few days," Sir Nicolas said, "I realise he was a very possessive man. I suppose in a way he was afraid that I might not be wholeheartedly loyal to him or might deviate from the course he was determined I should take."

"The Premier Baronet of Great Britain!" Fenella said gently.

"Exactly," Sir Nicolas agreed. "It was drummed into my head from the time I was a baby that my blue blood made me superior to other people. I was not allowed to read fairy stories like other children. Instead I learnt the achievements of the Waringham's down the centuries, and of course the deeds of my mother's ancestors also of which my father was equally proud."

"I am so, so sorry for you!" Fenella said impulsively.

"I do not want your sympathy," Sir Nicolas replied, "I want your help. I want you to marry me, Fenella, and teach me how to enjoy myself. I can give you every material comfort that you could ever want, and you could give me so much that is far more important."

His voice deepened and Fenella realised a little of what it must cost him to speak like this to her.

She knew how reserved he was, how all his life he had been buttoned up and unable to express himself, controlled to the point when he must have thought any passionate emotion was slightly beneath his dignity.

And now as if some dam had burst within himself he laid his heart at her feet.

Instinctively, because she was so sorry, her fingers tightened on his.

"What can I . . . say to you . . . Sir Nicolas?" she asked.

"You will marry me?"

She shook her head.

"You know I cannot do that."

"Why not?"

"It is quite simple," she answered, "I do not love you. And I know that however kind you might be to me, however hard we would both try, you would never know real happiness with someone who did not love you for yourself."

"I had a feeling you would say that to me," Sir Nicolas said, "but let me try to make you love me. I will be very gentle with you, Fenella. I will give you all the things you have never had. I will protect you look after you, and I know that I will never love anyone in my whole life as I love you now."

Fenella drew in a deep breath.

"I am honoured and proud that you should say such things to me," she said, "but you know that, even while you say them, I cannot give you the answer that you want to hear."

"It is Corbury, is it not?" Sir Nicolas asked.

"I have loved Periquine ever since I was a child," Fenella answered. "But he has no idea of it, and as you well know he is in love with Hetty."

"How can he be such a fool when he might have you?" Sir Nicolas asked.

"You must be blind if you ask that question," Fenella replied.

"Do you really think that Hetty with her affectations, her ambitions, her scheming and her all too obvious flirtations, can hold a candle to you?"

Sir Nicolas lifted her hand as he spoke and raised it to his lips.

"I never knew a woman could be so soft and sweet and feminine," he said, "and at the same time so gay and gallant."

"Please do not talk to me like that," Fenella pleaded, "you make me want to cry! Oh, Nicolas, I wish I could love you, I like you so much. I want you as a friend, and I shall pray that one day you will find a woman who will love you as much as you love her."

"I want you," Sir Nicolas said obstinately.

His eyes sought Fenella's and she was amazed to see how love had softened his hard features and the tight line of his mouth.

He looked different, human, and his pomposity had vanished. He was just a man sincerely and very much in love.

For a moment Fenella thought how comfortable life would be with him. He would be a considerate husband, she thought, and perhaps a very appreciative one.

Once the barriers with which he had surrounded himself were down, he would be ready to give the woman he loved a gentleness, an understanding, and perhaps a deep passion he was not yet aware of in himself.

Then Fenella saw Periquine's eyes and face, heard the note in his voice as he ordered her about, felt again that strange, rapturous, ecstatic thrill that had run through her as his lips touched hers.

"I am sorry . . . Nicolas, so very . . . very . . . sorry," she whispered.

He gave a deep sigh.

"I expected it," he said, "but I shall go on trying, Fenella. Perhaps one day you will need me and when you do I shall be there."

He kissed her hand again and rose to his feet.

"I will come back and see you this afternoon. At this moment I have strict instructions from your maid not to stay too long and overtire you."

"You have not done that," Fenella said, "and thank you for being so kind to me."

"I love you," he said looking down at her, with a sudden light in his eyes. "Never forget that, I love you."

He turned to walk away across the lawn and Fenella sinking back against the cushions wondered for a moment if she had dreamt the whole conversation.

Could it be true that Sir Nicolas Waringham, one of the richest men in England and quite the proudest, had asked her to be his wife and she had refused him?

It was true, but she knew that no-one, least of all Hetty, would believe that was what had occurred.

She was still thinking of Sir Nicolas when her heart gave a sudden leap as she saw Lord Corbury coming across the lawn from the house.

It was impossible not to admire the manner in which he moved, the way he carried his head, and his almost perfect athletic figure from his broad shoulders to his narrow hips.

He appeared as elegantly dressed as Sir Nicolas, and only Fenella's sharp eye noted a slight tear in the frill of his cravat, a crease in the arm of his coat which old Barnes had not been able to iron out, and that his boots were not polished as brightly as she would have wished.

But she was overwhelmingly glad to see him and it made her eyes sparkle and there was a smile on her lips as she held out her right hand to him.

"I was hoping you would come," she said.

"I came to show you this," Lord Corbury said and put the newspaper he carried into her hand.

"What is it?" she asked apprehensively.

It was unlike Periquine to sound so abrupt or to omit to enquire after her health.

"Read the bottom of the second column on the front page," he said harshly.

Fenella opened out the paper and found the item to which he referred. Slowly her spirits dropping, she read:

SMUGGLED CARGO DISCOVERED

Preventive vessels patrolling the South Coast, and the Dragon Guards searching for Smugglers yesterday discovered a boat sunk in Hellingly Creek. It contained a number of tubs of brandy and in several nearby caves there was also found many large bales of tobacco.

The military had on Tuesday night apprehended a dozen ponies which they suspected of making for Hellingly Creek to pick up a cargo.

The Smugglers however sank the boat before they could be apprehended, and two men suspected of being concerned in the carrying of contraband goods escaped on horse-back.

Fenella read the paragraph through twice before she said:

"So it was all for . . . nothing."

"Hardly nothing!" Lord Corbury retorted. "The whole operation cost nearly £ 1,500."

"As much as that?"

"What do you expect?" he asked harshly. "One can hardly expect it to have cost much less!"

Fenella sighed.

"I am sorry Periquine."

"It is just cursed bad luck," he said. "We actually

brought the cargo into the creek. Another half an hour
and we could have got it away to London."

"Not if they had apprehended the ponies."

"Curse it! Soldiers should be fighting wars, not
running round after a lot of petty thieves."

"We should be thankful we got off so easily,"
Fenella said. "It might have been much worse!"

As she spoke Lord Corbury's eyes went to her
arm and he said more gently:

"You might have been killed! Forgive me, Fenella, I should have asked you first how you were, but
as it happens Anna had already told me."

"I guessed that," Fenella said, "and I am sure
she gave you a scolding at the same time."

"A scolding!"

Lord Corbury put up his hands in horror.

"Do not speak to me of all the things that Anna
has said to me these past two days! I felt at any
moment I might be sent back to school with a re-
quest to the Head Master to punish me for my mis-
demeanours!"

"Anna has always been the same," Fenella said,
"she loves us both so much that she goes about in a
state of terror in case either of us should break our
necks."

Lord Corbury sat down on the seat recently va-
cated by Sir Nicolas.

"You know I would not have had it happen to
you for the world, Fenella," he said. "It was very
sporting of you to come with me, and I am grateful.
Even though we did not pull anything off."

"As you say, it was bad luck," Fenella said lightly.

"But I have an idea!"

"Another one?" Fenella enquired apprehensively.

"It is something quite different," he replied. "The
only thing is you have to promise me on your honour
you will not mention it to Waringham."

Fenella had no time to answer before he added:

"By the way, what the hell was Waringham doing here? I saw his Phaeton leaving as I rode across
the Park."

"He . . . he came to enquire how I was," Fenella answered. "Someone must have told him that I was not . . . well."

"Blast the fellow, why can he not go back to London?" Lord Corbury complained. "If I go to see Hetty, he is always there. I come to see you and I find him snooping round the place. I hope you are not encouraging him, Fenella. After all there is no point now in pretending to take an interest in his boring family tree."

"No . . . of course . . . not," Fenella said faintly.

"Now what I have learnt concerns Waringham, but it is absolutely essential that he should not hear a whisper of it. Do you promise me not to mention it to him?"

"Of course I will promise anything if you wish me to," Fenella replied.

"I trust you," Lord Corbury said. "Now this is what we are going to do. We are going to Ascot next week, and we are going to put all the money we have left on Waringham's horse 'Crusader'."

Fenella looked at Lord Corbury with startled eyes.

"Do you think it is going to win?" she asked.

"I know it is."

"But why then is it a secret from Sir Nicolas?"

"Because," Lord Corbury answered, "he is running two horses in the same race. His groom told Joe Jarvis when he was at 'The Green Man' and Jarvis told me because he thought I would be interested that the stable intend 'Crusader' to win, while 'Ivanhoe' Waringham's other horse, is at the moment the favourite for 'The Gold Cup'."

"Can they really arrange things like that?" Fenella asked.

"It has been done before," Lord Corbury replied. "The grooms, the stable lads, even the trainers, sometimes want to make a killing for themselves, and that I imagine is what they intend to do in this particular race."

"But surely Sir Nicolas must have some idea that it might happen," Fenella enquired.

"He knows what his trainer wants him to know," Lord Corbury replied, "and 'Ivanhoe' is a magnificent horse, there is no doubt about that. Everyone has been saying for months that it will win the 'Cup'."

He drew a deep breath.

" 'Crusader' is unknown and they expect him to start at ten to one, if not at longer odds. Do you realise what that means, Fenella?"

"What does it mean?" she asked, trying to understand exactly what Periquine was telling her.

"We have about £4,000 left in the Priest's Hole," Lord Corbury said impressively. "If 'Crusader' wins at no more than ten to one, that is £40,000. Think of it, Fenella! We have a tip straight from the stable. I am quite certain that his is where we make a fortune once and for all."

"I hope so, Periquine," Fenella said softly, "I do hope so."

"One gets information like this once in a lifetime," Lord Corbury said enthusiastically. "I did not intend to go to Ascot, I thought it would be too expensive, but I am certainly not going to miss seeing 'Crusader' romp home with all my money on his back."

"You are not thinking of going there just for the day?" Fenella asked.

"No, no, we will do it in style," Lord Corbury replied, "and stay with your uncle."

"With Uncle Roderick?" Fenella enquired.

"Why not?" Lord Corbury asked. "He is also my cousin, remember, and he has often said to me, 'If ever you come to Ascot for the races, dear boy, stay with me'. Write too him, Fenella, and tell him we shall both be arriving on the morning of the 'Gold Cup'."

He sighed:

"I would like to go for the whole meeting, but quite frankly I am frightened of fittering the money away on some of the other races. You know how hard it is not to bet when someone gives you 'a certainty'."

"I do not think that would be at all wise," Fenella agreed.

"It certainly would not, for our nest-egg is getting low," Lord Corbury said. "We have wasted too much on this last disaster. £1,500 is a hell of a lot of money! If you ask me, Renshaw should have warned us that the odds were against getting a boat into Hellingly. I have been hearing now that they have a whole armada of ships patrolling that part of the coast and the Dragoons are out every night."

"I did tell you they were making a special effort to stop the smuggling traffic across the Channel," Fenella reminded him.

"It is no use crying over spilt milk!" Lord Corbury said with a characteristic change of voice. "We have had the good fortune to hear about this particular horse and we would be fools not to take advantage of such knowledge."

He paused and then he said:

"£40,000! I like the sound of it!"

"Would you . . . then be able to . . . offer for . . . Hetty?" she enquired hesitatingly.

"I should certainly feel more in a position to do so," Lord Corbury replied.

He rose to his feet as he spoke and said casually:

"Are you coming over to the Priory this afternoon?"

"I would like to," Fenella answered, "but I doubt if Anna will let me. I will come tomorrow."

"I have missed you."

"Have you . . . have you really?"

She looked up at him but he was not looking down at her as she had hoped. Instead he was staring across the lawn with a rather strange expression on his face.

"£40,000!" he said again almost beneath his breath.

She knew with a little pain in her heart that he was not thinking of her.

Chapter Eight

"CAN I speak to you, Papa?"

The Honourable Lionel Lambert looked up from his book and replied irritably:

"You can see I am busy!"

"I am sorry, Papa, but I must interrupt you."

Fenella closed the door behind her and walked towards her father. He was seated at his big desk which was covered with books.

There were in fact books everywhere. Books lining the walls, books piled on the side-tables, books stacked on the floor. There was no room for doubt to anyone entering the room where its owner's interests lay.

"I have no time for conversation at this moment," the Honourable Lionel said positively, "and I suspect that once again, Fenella, you have come to ask me for money."

"Yes I have, Papa, and please understand I would not worry you if it were not of great import."

"You always say that," her father retorted.

"Periquine and I are going to Ascot to stay with Uncle Roderick for the races," Fenella said, "and, Papa, I really have nothing to wear! I cannot go to Ascot like this, can I?"

As she spoke she held out the skirt of her cotton dress then looked at her father with a pleading expression on her face.

"Clothes! clothes! That is all women ever think

141

of!" he said crossly. "If ever there was a waste of money it is expending it on gowns which are out of fashion before they are worn out, or on frills and furbelows which do little to enhance real beauty. The Greeks found them unnecessary."

"All the same, I expect the Greek women wished to look their best for the Games, or whatever it was they went to," Fenella replied.

Her father did not answer and coaxingly she said:

"If I were a boy, Papa, I would be far more expensive, you know that!"

"If I had had a son," the Honourable Lionel Lambert said, "that would have been very different. He would have gone to Eton and then to Oxford, as I did. He would have taken his degree and then we would have been able to travel together.

"We would have gone to Greece and seen where Homer wrote 'The Iliad' and 'The Odyssey'. We could have admired together the perfection of the Parthenon and the Propylaea built by Pericles to proclaim his 'full democracy'."

He gave a deep sigh.

"There would have been many things which would have been of interest to us both. But then I never had a son!"

There was so much feeling in his voice that Fenella could not answer.

She realised for the first time how deeply disappointed her father must have been when she had been born and he had learnt afterwards that her mother could never have another child.

All these years, she thought to herself, he must have resented the fact that she was of the wrong sex.

The reason he grudged her new gowns and anything that appertained to femininity was that he would have so willingly spent a hundred times more on the education and upbringing of a son!

Impulsively Fenella bent forward and kissed her father's cheek.

"I am sorry I am such a disappointment," she said softly.

"You are nothing of the sort," her father replied rather inconvincingly.

He put his fingers in his waistcoat pocket and brought out some sovereigns. He counted them out on the desk. There were five of them.

"That will get you what you need, Fenella."

Then as if he was no longer interested in her, his eyes went back to his book.

Fenella had opened her lips to say that five pounds would not be enough for what she required, but realised she could not plead any more with him.

She understood now so much that had bewildered her before: the manner in which her father had always been ready to expend money on horses and books, on the up-keep of the house and the estate, but invariably cheesepared and grumbled at anything that was necessary where she was concerned.

She was a girl and he had wanted so desperately that she should be a boy!

As she went from the Library with the sovereigns in her hand, Fenella was thinking not of herself and the problem of what she should wear to go to Ascot, but of her father finding his only solace and happiness in reading, while her mother expended all her energy and interest in the garden.

It was a strange marriage, she thought, and yet in some ways they seemed content with each other. It was only where she was concerned that they both seemed to have a blind spot.

She gave a little sigh and then because, as Anna would have said, "What can't be cured must be endured," she tried to think how she could manage to buy almost an entire wardrobe with five pounds.

The very least she required was a dress with a light silk coat to wear over it, a bonnet, gloves and shoes to wear at the races, and an evening gown for dinner.

How could she manage? How was it possible to

procure all those things with just five golden sovereigns?

Then she could hear Periquine's voice saying enthusiastically:

"'Crusader' is unknown and they expect him to start at ten to one, if not longer odds!"

If she wagered £5 at ten to one, she would win £50! Here, Fenella thought, was the solution to her problem.

With £50 she could buy clothes that for once would make her look attractive, which would make Periquine proud of her. She could not go to the races feeling that girls like Hetty were looking at her with contempt, or fearing that Periquine would have to apologise for his poor shabby little cousin.

£50! It was a fortune, and just for once perhaps Periquine would look at her with that glint of admiration in his eyes which he invariably reserved for Hetty.

The road into Ascot was crowded with every sort of vehicle.

There were phaetons, chaises, landaus, barouches, tilburys, gigs, large coaches packed with noisy and enthusiastic race-goers, and crowds of pedestrians on foot, all making their way in a holiday mood towards the Stands gleaming white in the summer sunshine beside the smooth green track.

Sitting beside Lord Corbury in his phaeton, Fenella felt more excited as every minute passed.

She was well aware that many people looked at them admiringly and it was true that they made a singularly handsome couple. Moreover Lord Corbury's horse-flesh was also beyond criticism.

Fenella had felt that her cup of happiness almost over-flowed when he fetched her from the Hall at a very early hour. She had seen as she came down the steps to where he was waiting, an undoubted expression of admiration before he ejaculated:

"Good Heavens, Fenella, you are so smart I did not recognise you!"

She would not have been honest with herself if she did not realise that she was in fact looking unusually attractive in a gown of daffodil yellow with a silk coat to match, trimmed with pearl buttons and white braid.

Her chip-straw bonnet was decorated with yellow kingcups and it tied under her small chin with satin ribbons of the same colour.

It accentuated the purity of her skin and brought out the red lights in her hair. But it was in fact the excitement and look of happiness in her green eyes and the smile on her lips which made people who looked at her turn to look again.

Lord Corbury himself was not to be outdone in splendour.

When Fenella had gone to Brighton and bought her gowns at a shop where, because they knew her mother, she could obtain credit, she had expended some of her precious money in buying a new cravat for him.

Starched and frilled, it was snowy against his sun-burnt chin, and with his exquisitely cut coat fitting without a wrinkle across his broad shoulders, his Hessian boots shining so brightly that passing traffic was reflected in them, and with his high hat worn at an angle, Fenella was sure that every woman on the Race course who saw him would envy her for being in his company.

Lord Corbury had transferred the gold from the Priest's Hole into notes and received a good price for it.

That had put him into a good temper, and when Fenella asked him a little hesitantly if he would mind wagering her humble £5 at the same time as his own, he had agreed without the arguments she had expected.

She did not tell him that it was all she possessed or that she had not paid for her clothes. She thought if she did so he would feel obliged to offer her some of his winnings and that she would not accept.

"He is doing all this for Hetty," she told herself, "and I would not touch that money, not if I was starving in the gutter!"

She told herself, as she had done so often before, that it was small and petty of her to be jealous of Hetty.

Yet when they walked across the green lawns and saw Hetty coming towards them, it was impossible for Fenella to feel anything but her usual helpless inferiority.

If she was pretty in her new daffodil yellow gown, Hetty was looking radiantly beautiful in a soft strawberry pink ensemble that showed up the fairness of her skin and hair, and made her look like a rosebud.

"Periquine! How delightful to see you!" she said to Lord Corbury holding out the small white gloved hand and raising her china-blue eyes to his with a gesture which was calculated to send any impressionable young man into a fever of delight.

Fenella looked away. Somehow she could not bear to see the expression on Periquine's face.

She felt the happiness and elation that had been hers ever since they left home, ebb away from her.

"Perhaps after today," she told herself, "Periquine will be in a position to ask Sir Virgil for Hetty's hand in marriage!" "Then it would not matter what she wore or what she did, Periquine would be lost to her!"

It was with a slight feeling of comfort that she saw Sir Nicolas approaching.

"I was not expecting to see you here today," he said as he reached her side, "you did not tell me you were coming."

"Periquine made up his mind only at the last moment," Fenella answered uncomfortably.

She knew that Sir Nicolas would think it strange when she appeared at Ascot, but she had not warned him of their intention to be present lest Periquine should think she was betraying his interest in the horse they were to back.

Looking up into Sir Nicolas's face she wondered if in fact Periquine's information was correct.

Could it be possible that Sir Nicolas's stable of all stables would do anything that was even slightly crooked, or arrange a race so that an outsider won rather than the favourite?

Then she told herself that it was too late to ask questions or to do anything but acquiesce in Periquine's plans.

"Come and look at the horses in the paddock," Sir Nicolas suggested.

Fenella knew it was because he wanted to talk to her alone. She glanced at Lord Corbury to see him deep in conversation with Hetty and her escort. Because she felt forgotten, Fenella said quickly:

"I would like that."

"Did you get my letter?" Sir Nicolas asked as they moved away.

"I have had three letters from you," Fenella answered, "since you left the Hall."

"And you have not answered one of them."

"I have been meaning to, but I have had so much to do these last few days."

"Looking after Corbury, I suppose," Sir Nicolas said bitterly.

It was the truth and Fenella did not deny it.

She had been getting Periquine's clothes ready, tidying the Priory and finding that because her arm still hurt her a little, she grew tired rather easily.

When she returned home she had been glad to flop into bed and be fussed over by Anna rather than sit down and answer letters.

Besides it was very difficult to know what to say in answer to Sir Nicolas's protestations of love.

She had not imaged he would be so romantic or indeed so poetical, but she had learnt now that, while he found it difficult to say the things he felt in his heart, he could pour them out on paper and be in fact very eloquent.

"My letters do not bore you?" he asked suddenly, and she saw by the expression on his face that he was afraid of her answer.

"No of course not," she said gently, "I am proud that you should want to write to me and I value your letters."

"Is that the truth?" he enquired.

"I promise you one thing," Fenella answered, "I will never lie to you."

Even as she spoke she felt a little guilty. She was not lying to him, but she was keeping something from him that she thought he ought to know.

Then she knew that she could not under any circumstances betray Periquine's secret.

She changed the subject and discussed the horses. Sir Nicolas was very knowledgeable on the subject and when they strolled back from the paddock towards the lawns below the Royal Box he said:

"I shall not bet on this race, but I intend to back my own horse for the Gold Cup. I want you to see 'Ivanhoe', he is a magnificent beast."

It was with great difficulty that Fenella repressed an inclination to advise him not to bet on his own horse.

But even as she played with the idea, Lord Corbury joined them and she saw from the look in his eyes that something had pleased him.

"I want to show you something, Fenella," he said, and with a smile at Sir Nicolas she walked away with him to another part of the lawn.

"Joe Jarvis is here," Lord Corbury said in a conspiratorial whisper, "I have just had a word with him."

"What did he say?" Fenella asked.

"It is all arranged exactly as we expected. He has had a talk with the groom who gave him the information in the first place, and the whole of Sir Nicolas's stable are backing 'Crusader'."

"Have you put your money on yet?"

"I have put every penny I possess and your money on 'Crusader'. They think it will start a little higher than ten to one, so I did not take a price."

"Oh, Periquine, I hope it is all right!" Fenella hardly breathed the words.

"Of course it is all right," he answered, "it has to be!"

He smiled down at her gaily.

"It is 'win all or lose all' where we are concerned, but personally I feel extremely confident."

Fenella laughed.

"You are always the same, Periquine! You always believe fervently in your own luck and sometimes it comes off."

"It always comes off!" he boasted. "We may have lost money on our last adventure, but do not forget we saved our lives. As you have pointed out so often to me, there is nothing so valuable."

"No indeed," Fenella agreed.

"Let us keep our fingers crossed and say a special prayer to the god of racing, whoever he may be!" Lord Corbury smiled.

Then a friend came up to speak to him and there was no chance for any further private conversation.

They went down to the paddock together to look at the horses parading in the ring.

"Ivanhoe" was certainly an outstanding animal. Everyone was admiring him but Fenella had eyes only for "Crusader." He was long legged and somewhat gawky in appearance, but she had the feeling that he would show both stamina and speed once he was on the course.

She watched Sir Nicolas's jockeys wearing his colours of dark blue and gold mount, and then the horses proceeded past the Royal Box and cantered away to the start.

They walked back to the lawns. Fenella saw Sir Nicolas looking in her direction, but she pretended not to see him.

She knew this was a moment so tense, so important both to her and to Periquine, that she could not bear to have anyone else standing with them.

They moved down almost to the rails. She heard

a sudden murmur from the crowd the cry of "They're off!" and knew the race had started.

Periquine had told her to keep her fingers crossed. She did that and now she started to will the horse into the lead.

" 'Crusader' win, you must win."

She tried not to think that £40,000 would mean that Periquine would be able to marry Hetty.

She tried to think how much it would mean to him to be free of debt, to know that he could repair the Priory, could live comfortably and without scrounging round in all sorts of ridiculous and dangerous ways to make money.

" 'Crusader' win, you must win! You must!"

The horses were coming down the straight. Every head was turned left to watch them. Now they were in sight and Fenella could see the jockey's colours quite clearly.

"First time round," Lord Corbury remarked tersely. "It is a two and half mile race."

The horses passed them all bunched together. "Ivanhoe" and "Crusader" were quite close to each other.

On the far side of the course, the horses began to stretch out. There was one several lengths ahead for a short time, but it was soon overtaken.

Now they were on the straight again. There were two horses in front and on one there was not mistaking a blue and gold cap!

They were coming nearer and nearer, and now it looked as if there would be a neck and neck finish between the two leading animals.

Nearer and nearer! It was impossible for Fenella to see anything but the Jockey's colours or to know whether it was "Ivanhoe" or "Crusader" which was ahead.

With a roar from the crowd the horses passed the post. Sir Nicolas had won! There was no doubt that his colours had been carried half a length ahead of any other horse.

Then Fenella saw coming in fourth or perhaps

fifth the same blue and gold cap and this time she could see more clearly. There was no doubt that "Ivanhoe" was the winner!

She gave a little gasp, but before she could say anything, before she could even ask the question to which she already knew the answer, she saw the darkness on Lord Corbury's face and the rage in his expression.

He turned without a word and walked across the lawns towards the enclosure where the jockeys would unsaddle and weigh in, and because there was nothing else she could do, Fenella followed him.

As they got there, the horses were coming in from the course. "Ivanhoe" came first amid cheers and hand-clapping.

"Well done! A fine race! Ye did well, boy!"

People were reaching out to pat the horse as it passed. Lord Corbury stood watching. Then he said abruptly, his voice thick with anger:

"Stay here! I will find out what happened."

He disappeared into the crowd moving towards the weighing-in room.

Fenella walked slowly away to stand under the trees which bordered the course. There was no-one there to pay any attention to her and she stood wondering what had gone wrong and what Periquine would do now.

She was certain that he had done as he said and put every penny he possessed on the horse. Now they had nothing left.

There would be no money to pay Porrit for doing the repairs to the farm, no money to provide Mrs. Buckle and Barnes with their wages, no money for food, and she remembered too that she would have no money to pay for the clothes she had bought in Brighton on credit!

What was more she had not even kept anything back to tip the servants at her Uncle's house!

She felt suddenly sick, not only at what had happened, but because she and Periquine had been so stupid.

Why had they risked everything instead of being more cautious and wagering only half their money? If only Periquine had set out to win £20,000 instead of £40,000, he would now at least have £2,000 left for every-day expenses.

"We were mad!" she told herself and wondered why she had not tried to persuade him into being more sensible.

"I am as foolish as he is," she thought.

But that was poor consolation when the future seemed dark and hopeless and there appeared to be at the moment nothing they could do about it.

She heard a bell ring and knew the weighing-in had been completed and the next race would soon be starting.

There was no sign of Periquine, and there was nothing she could do but wait for him and hope she would find some way of consoling him when he did appear.

The horses left the paddock for the last race. Fenella watched them gallop down the course and wondered why anyone was so stupid as to put their money on anything so chancy as a horse-race.

"It was just as stupid," she thought, "as gaming at cards when inevitably sooner or later one is the loser."

The race finished and she heard the cheers for the winner, but there was still no sign of Periquine.

It was then she heard someone approaching and looked round quickly to see Sir Nicolas.

"Whatever are you doing here," he asked. "I have been looking for you everywhere."

"I am waiting for Periquine," she answered.

"Alone?" he enquired. "You know perfectly well, Fenella, he should not leave you unaccompanied on a race-course."

"I am all right," she answered.

"That is not the point," Sir Nicolas said stiffly. "Come along. I will take you to your Uncle's. I imagine you are staying with him."

"I must wait for Periquine."

"Why?" he enquired. "He appears to have forgotten your existence. How long have you been here?"

"Not very . . . long."

"Long enough! I will not have you hanging about waiting for that young waster when he has not the decency to look after you as he should."

"I must wait for him," Fenella said, "he told me he would come back."

"It is impossible for you to stay here," Sir Nicolas said as if reasoning with a child. "You will get yourself talked about, Fenella, Come, take my arm and I will escort you to my chaise."

"No, Nicolas," Fenella protested.

He put out his hand and took hers.

"I insist! It is not only insulting for you to have to stand here alone, it is unconventional and I will not allow it."

He pulled her forward as he spoke and she pulled against him.

"No, Nicolas, no! I must wait!"

"What is going on?" a voice asked angrily.

Fenella and Sir Nicolas looked round to see that Lord Corbury had approached them unexpectedly.

"Here you are, Periquine!" Fenella cried in relief. "I thought you had forgotten all about me."

"I was detained," Lord Corbury replied briefly, "and may I ask why Waringham is behaving in this unaccountable manner?"

"I was persuading Fenella that it is both incorrect and unconventional for her to wait here alone," Sir Nicolas said in icy tones. "Something you appear to have over-looked!"

"It is not your business," Lord Corbury replied rudely, "and I resent your pulling my cousin about, in the same manner that you undoubtedly pulled your second horse in the 'Gold Cup'."

Lord Corbury spoke furiously although his voice was low, but there was no doubt that he had lost his temper. Fenella gave a little gasp as Sir Nicolas said slowly in even tones:

"I consider that an insult."

"That is exactly what I meant it to be!" Lord Corbury retorted.

"I think, Corbury, it is time you were taught a lesson," Sir Nicolas answered, "and I shall have much pleasure in blowing a hole through you tomorrow morning at dawn."

"No! no!" Fenella cried.

But neither of the men facing each other with hatred in their expressions paid any attention to her.

"I accept your invitation with pleasure," Lord Corbury said sarcastically. "My seconds shall wait on yours within a few hours and I can promise you, Waringham, that if anyone learns a lesson, it will be you."

"That of course remains to be seen," Sir Nicolas replied, his voice entirely expressionless.

He bowed stiffly to Fenella and walked away, his shoulders and the carriage of his head eloquent with his disapproval of what had taken place.

"Periquine, you cannot fight him! You must not!" Fenella cried.

"Blow a hole through me!" Lord Corbury exclaimed in disgust. "I will blow a hole through him and I hope it kills him!"

"Periquine, you are mad! You cannot do such a thing!"

"I can and I will!" Lord Corbury retorted. "It is entirely his fault we have lost our money."

"Why?" Fenella enquired.

"Because he changed the jockey on 'Crusader' just before the race. No-one knows why he did it. They do not think he had a suspicion that anything was afoot. But nevertheless he gave his orders and there was no question of their being disobeyed."

"You mean it might have been chance?"

"Much as I loathe Waringham, I have to be frank and admit that is what everyone concerned thinks it was!" Lord Corbury answered. "In fact it was just damn bad luck!"

He pressed his lips together and squared his chin.

"Come on, there is nothing to be gained by talk-ing about it. We have to face facts, we are broke, completely and absolutely rolled up."

He walked across the paddock moving swiftly while Fenella struggled to keep up with him.

They found their phaeton and drove in silence towards Lord Farquhar's house which was only half a mile away from the race-course.

Just before they turned in at the drive, Fenella said miserably:

"I am sorry, Periquine, about ... the duel."

"Sorry!" he ejaculated sharply. "So you should be! You have encouraged Waringham to make a cake of himself from the very first!"

"I ... did not ... mean ... to do so," Fenella protested.

She saw by the expression on Lord Corbury's face that he was incensed with her.

She would have pleaded with him, but at that moment he drew up the horses outside the front door of Lord Farquhar's residence.

She alighted and the servants removed their va-lises from beneath the phaeton. Raising his hat Lord Corbury said coldly:

"Goodbye, Fenella."

"Where are you going?" she asked hastily.

"I have business to attend to," he replied frigidly. "Will you give your uncle my respects and say I shall unfortunately not be dining with him tonight as I intended, but will hope to see him before he retires."

"But Periquine, surely...." Fenella began.

But already Lord Corbury was moving his horses and her words were lost.

She knew then that he was going to find sec-onds for the duel he was to fight at dawn with Sir Nicolas.

She knew too that he was blue-devilled at what had occurred and the only solace he was likely to find was drinking with any of his friends who would be obliging enough to pay.

"He is in worse trouble than ever before!" Fenella thought, "and it is all my fault!"

As she walked into the hall she felt the tears welling into her eyes and found her Uncle, tall and distinguished if slightly rotund in his middle age, waiting to greet her.

"I am delighted to see you, Fenella, my dear. ..." he began. Then he saw the tears.

"What has happened?" he asked.

"Oh, Uncle Roderick," Fenella replied. "Everything has gone wrong. It has been such a . . . horrible . . . day!"

Her voice broke on the last words and the tears ran down her face. She hardly realised what was happening as Lord Farquhar led her into the Salon and sat her down on the sofa.

Old bachelor though he was, he was experienced enough in the female sex to know exactly what to do when a lady wept.

He took off Fenella's bonnet, untying the yellow ribbons skilfully, and produced a large soft linen handkerchief before putting his arm round her he let her cry on his shoulder.

"There, there," he said soothingly, "tell me what has happened, it cannot be as bad as all that."

"It is! It is worse!" Fenella sobbed. "Periquine has lost all his money . . . every penny, and now he has . . . quarrelled with Sir Nicolas over . . . me and they are going to fight a . . . duel.

"I know there is . . . nothing I can do to . . . stop them, as I could not bear Nicolas to . . . hurt Periquine or indeed for Periquine to hurt . . . Nicolas! What is more I have not . . . paid for my own . . . gowns and Papa will be so . . . angry."

Fenella's voice became quite incoherent and Lord Farquhar wisely let her cry without questioning her further for the moment.

When at last she became a little more composed, even to the extent of blowing her nose fiercely on his handkerchief, he said:

"Now tell me everything from the very beginning."

"If I do," Fenella said weakly, "you will not be ... angry with ... Periquine?"

"Why should I be?" Lord Farquhar asked. "I promise you I find him a very engaging young man."

"I felt you would ... understand, Uncle Roderick," Fenella said. "You were always so ... kind to me when I was a little ... girl, I used to love it when you came to stay."

"And how can I help you now?" Lord Farquhar asked.

"You cannot ... no-one can," Fenella answered miserably. "Periquine and I are in a terrible tangle ... and I cannot ... see anyway ... out."

"Suppose I try to find one," Lord Farquhar suggested.

"I think it is ... impossible," Fenella murmured forlornly.

Nevertheless encouraged by such sympathy and with some skilful prompting she told her Uncle everything that had happened from the moment Periquine came home from the Army.

She did not speak of her love for him, but she had no idea how revealing her voice was when she spoke of his affection for Hetty, or how desperate she sounded when she recounted what had happened when Periquine had deliberately provoked Sir Nicolas to a duel.

"Can you not ... stop them ... Uncle Roderick?"

"No-one can stop a duel of honour, my dear," he replied, "but I have a suspicion that by the time they have cooled down a little and discovered that five o'clock in the morning is a most unsalubrious time for being emotional, the results will not be as bad as you anticipate."

"You do not ... think Nicolas will ... hurt Periquine?"

"Not mortally at any rate," Lord Farquhar said dryly. "Waringham has far too much a sense of consequence to wish to flee the country for several years and I doubt if Periquine has any real desire to murder anyone."

"I hope . . . you are . . . right," Fenella said in a small voice.

"And now what are we to do about you and your burden of debts?" Lord Farquhar inquired with a hint of laughter in his voice.

"Papa will be furious!" Fenella sighed. "He gave me five pounds, which you well know was not enough, but I did not like to plague him for more. You see, Uncle Roderick, I have only just realised that Papa is bitterly disappointed that I am not a boy! He wanted a son, and I suppose he will never forgive me for not being one."

Lord Farquhar was silent for a moment and then he said:

"I see I have been rather amiss, Fenella, in not paying more attention to you this last year or so since you grew up. I think the time has come for me to act as an uncle should and take you under my wing. Perhaps I better constitute myself as your Guardian. After all there is some sense in that."

"It would be wonderful!" Fenella cried. "But I am sure you do not wish to be troubled with me."

"On the contary," Lord Farquhar replied, "you could so easily have been my daughter and every time I see you I wish you were."

Fenella looked at him with bright eyes.

"You mean that you . . . wanted to marry . . . Mama."

Lord Farquhar smiled.

"She preferred your father," he said simply. "I can never understand why!"

Fenella gave a little laugh.

"If you cannot be my father, Uncle Roderick, I am so very glad you are my only and quite my most favourite Uncle."

He bent to kiss her cheek.

"You and I will have to put our heads together and see what we can do about these young men of yours. You do not wish to marry Waringham?"

"No."

"A pity—but I suppose you are in love with Periquine."

Fenella sighed.

"Is it so obvious? He must never know I love him! You see he does not care about me, he wants to marry Hetty Baldwyn."

"Well, knowing Sir Virgil and his mercenary interests," Lord Farquhar said, "I reckon there is at this moment about as much chance of that as of Periquine jumping over the moon."

"I know," Fenella answered, "and that is what makes him so unhappy! That is why he wanted £40,000!"

"He certainly went about getting his money in a somewhat reprehensible manner," Lord Farquhar said. "At the same time it may have all been a good experience. I am only thankful I do not have to save you both from being transported."

"Could you have done so?" Fenella asked.

"It might have been possible," Lord Farquhar replied with a twinkle in his eye. "At the same time it is something I would rather not attempt."

Fenella laughed.

"You are such a comfort, Uncle Roderick," she said. "I am desperately worried about Periquine."

"I am sure you are," Lord Farquhar replied, "but nevertheless I hope it will not prevent you from looking your best at dinner tonight; for I have asked a number of very charming people to meet you."

"I am sure that will be most enjoyable!" Fenella answered.

At the same time she knew miserably that however interesting the people might be, her thoughts would stray all the time to Periquine.

He would be in the depths of despair, and however much he might be seeking to drown his sorrows, he would, she knew, although he would never admit it, be apprehensive as to what would happen at dawn tomorrow.

Chapter Nine

It was cold and dank in the wood.

It had not been difficult for Fenella to find out where the duels, which apparently were quite prevalent at Ascot, took place.

She had merely had to ask the Gentleman who had sat next to her at dinner the previous night where such dramatic incidents were enacted, and he had told her that Shepherd's Wood was the regular rendez-vous of those who had challenged each other.

"It is also notable for suicides," he said cheerily, "but as Ascot has not such a long history as Newmarket or Epsom, we have not had so many of those."

"I am glad to hear it," Fenella said fervently.

"The duellists are a different kettle of fish," he went on. "Owners are always falling out regarding the merits of their horses or accusing each other of shady practices, and such allegations invariably involve the use of pistols."

"Has anyone recently been badly . . . injured?" Fenella asked nervously.

"Sir Charles Cholmley lost an arm last year," her dinner partner said lightly, "but usually they inflict only superficial wounds. Or in some cases, if the antagonists have spent the night drinking, they miss each other altogether!"

He laughed heartily, but Fenella found it difficult to smile. She had said goodnight to her Uncle after the party had left, and as he kissed her, Lord Farquhar said:

"Do not worry unduly over that young scamp. I have known Periquine ever since he was born and I have never found him not to come out of a scrap smiling happily and quite surprised anyone should have been perturbed about him."

"I know," Fenella murmured, "but this is . . . different . . . somehow."

She told herself, when she got upstairs to her bed-room, it was different because she herself was involved.

She might have guessed, she thought, that sooner or later Sir Nicolas would seize an opportunity to fight Periquine.

She was well aware that not only was he jealous but he did in fact violently disapprove of Periquine's easy and irresponsible way of facing his problems and not making any proper attempt to overcome them.

He had already spoken to Fenella about the risks they had taken both in robbery and smuggling.

"You must have realised what would happen to you if you were caught!" he said.

She knew from the note in his voice that he was deeply perturbed about her.

"I did think of that," she answered, "but Periquine is always lucky."

"And what about you?" he had asked. "Do you think I could bear it if you were involved in a scandal or, worse still, taken before the Courts?"

Fenella had not answered and he had put his hand on hers and said:

"Promise me, please promise me that you will not do anything so foolhardy again."

"I will try not to," Fenella said.

She knew even as she spoke that if Periquine really wanted her, she would follow him whatever the cost to herself.

"If there is anything which involves you in danger," Sir Nicolas said, "I beg of you, Fenella, to tell me about it first. I swear to you I will not make trouble, but I will try to think of a solution without your being engaged in anything that might harm you."

She knew he was genuinely concerned on her behalf and somehow it was comforting to know how much she meant to him.

"I will tell you if it is . . . possible," she promised, "but if it is Periquine's secret, you know I must be . . . loyal to him."

He kissed her hand but she had seen the pain in his eyes.

She knew that he resented Lord Corbury's hold over her, while he was sensible enough to realise there was nothing he could do about it.

Now as she walked through the wood, Fenella wondered if anything could be worse than knowing the two men she cared for and who meant most in her life were about to try to injure each other, and that undoubtedly one of them would come off worse in the contest.

She found quite easily the clearing which her dinner partner had described to her.

It was about the size of a large ball room, encircled by trees and protected from prying eyes. With its flat surface of moss and sand it made a perfect arena for a duel.

At one side there was some thick rhododendron bushes, and Fenella realised that if she concealed herself in those she would be able to watch without being seen.

As she had left Lord Farquhar's house soon after 4 o'clock she reckoned that she would have at least half an hour's wait so having crawled into the bushes, she sat down in the centre of them and began to pray that neither Periquine nor Sir Nicolas would be hurt.

When she thought back about what had happened it all seemed so childish and absurd.

Yet she knew that fundamentally the roots of the quarrel lay in Sir Nicolas's disapproval and anger at Periquine having taken her into danger, and in

Periquine's envy of his wealth and his dislike of any suitor for Hetty's hand.

"Perhaps," Fenella thought, "it would have been wise to tell Periquine that Sir Nicolas is no longer interested in Hetty."

But she had felt shy of confessing that Sir Nicolas had asked her to marry him and, what was more important, she was not certain what Periquine's reaction would be to such information.

She seemed to have sat in the rhododendron bush for a long time before there was the sound of voices.

She heard a wheeled vehicle drive into the wood followed by another, and then first Sir Nicolas appeared with his seconds and almost immediately behind him Lord Corbury with two of his friends.

Both men were elegantly and flamboyantly dressed, unlike most duellists who wore dark shirts and black cravats so that they would not be an obvious target for their opponents.

The four seconds conferred with each other, but Fenella noticed that Lord Corbury made no effort to speak to Sir Nicolas, and the latter stood stiffly aside with a disdainful and contemptuous look on his face.

The box of duelling pistols was carried to the clearing by two grooms who then withdrew. Now the seconds were inspecting the weapons and balancing them to see they were in order.

There was the sound of another horse approaching, and a middle-aged man rode through the trees dismounted and came towards them.

"Good morning, Sir," Lord Corbury said to him, "it is very kind of you to get up so early in order to referee this Herculean contest."

"I agree with you," the newcomer said in a tired voice. "If there is one thing I dislike it is having to rise so early to see that two young fools at least keep to the rules of the game."

"We shall do that," Lord Corbury said sharply as if the newcomer had insulted him.

The Referee however ignored him and walking towards the seconds apparently had a great deal to say in a low voice which Fenella could not overhear.

At last Lord Corbury, as the one who had been challenged, chose his weapon and Sir Nicolas took the other pistol.

The seconds stood on each side of the clearing and the Referee took up his position.

"Now you both know the rules, Gentlemen," he said. "You will stand back to back, walk ten paces away from each other as I count, turn on my word of command and fire. Is that clear?"

"Quite clear," Sir Nicolas said in a quiet unemotional voice.

They took up their positions back to back and now Fenella clasping her hands together felt as if she could hardly breathe.

Periquine was so broad-shouldered, so large, she felt it was impossible for Sir Nicolas to miss him. Would he aim at his heart? Or would he be satisfied with just winging him in the arm?

Equally Nicolas himself with his starched white cravat and elegantly fitting grey coat would be an easy target for Periquine who was, she knew, an exceptional pistol shot.

"Please God do not let either of them be hurt!" she prayed. "Please God let them spare each other!"

Her fingers were so tightly clenched that her knuckles were white.

"Are you ready?" the Referee enquired.

She heard both contestants murmur in the affirmative.

"One," the Referee called, "two . . ."

Lord Corbury and Sir Nicolas started walking away from each other, but suddenly there was an interruption.

There was the sound of a carriage travelling at a great speed through the wood. A moment later a chaise drawn by two horses appeared through the trees. It was drawn sharply to a standstill and out jumped a radiant figure in a white evening gown.

It was only a short distance from the chaise to the centre of the duelling ground, and her white satin slippers sped over the moss so that in the space of a few seconds, even as the Referee intoned the fourth numeral that Hetty reached the very place where Lord Corbury and Sir Nicolas had been standing back to back.

"Stop!" she cried, "Stop!"

Her voice rang out and both the duellists turned round in astonishment.

Hetty was looking exceedingly beautiful, her fair hair vivid against the darkness of the trees, the diamonds round her neck sparkling in the first morning light, and Fenella realised that she must have come straight from a Ball because she was still in full evening dress.

Her tulle gown, flounced, frilled and bedecked with tiny bunches of rose-buds, was elaborate enough to grace any Assembly however distinguished.

"Stop!" Hetty cried again. "I will not have this! I will not allow you to fight over me!"

She flung out her arms dramatically.

"How can you be so selfish, so foolish," she enquired, "as not to realise that such a scandalous episode will damage my reputation?"

Both Lord Corbury and Sir Nicolas, having turned round on their tracks, were staring at her in stupefaction as she continued:

"I cannot imagine how either of you can be so inconsiderate! I will not allow you to fight and you will both stop immediately! Do you understand?"

Lord Corbury found his voice first.

"As it happens, Hetty," he said, "we are not fighting over you!"

For a moment it seemed as if Hetty did not understand him.

She was still standing with her arms out-stretched dramatically, but now her large blue eyes were on his face and she turned a little towards him.

"Not . . . fighting . . . over . . . me," she repeated slowly as if the words could not penetrate 'her mind.

"No," Lord Corbury replied, "it is in fact—some-one else."

"Another woman?! I do not believe it!" Hetty ejaculated.

She turned towards Sir Nicolas.

"Is Periquine lying?" she asked him. "I cannot be-lieve . . . I cannot credit for a moment . . . that either of . . . you would fight over . . . anyone else."

Her surprise was almost comic.

"It is true," Sir Nicolas said quietly. "You are not involved in any way in this disagreement be-tween Corbury and myself."

"You dare to tell me such a thing!" Hetty cried, and Fenella watching realised she had lost her tem-per.

She stamped her small foot on the mossy ground.

"You have the audacity to fight over someone else!" she exclaimed. "To make me a laughing-stock, when everyone knows that both of you have been dancing attendance on me for these past two months? I hate you, Periquine, do you hear, I hate you! And as for you, Sir Nicolas, I thought . . . I believed . . . you . . . cared for . . . me!"

She stamped her foot again, and then as if com-pletely losing control she stood there twisting her fingers together, apparently finding it impossible to express the anger that surged within her.

Because Fenella was sorry for Hetty, she rose in-voluntarily and without thinking from her hiding place to push her way through the bushes.

Even as she did so, Hetty with a last exclamation of fury turned on her heels and ran back towards the chaise.

The Gentleman who had brought her had not alighted from the vehicle but had sat during the whole proceeding holding his horses in check and being merely a spectator of the drama that was being un-folded in front of him.

Now when Hetty rejoined him and remounted the chaise, he realised that she wished to leave im-mediately and drove his horses away through the trees following a track which would eventually lead them to the other side of the wood.

Lord Corbury and Sir Nicolas, watching her go, stood as if frozen in their tracks, until as she disappeared they returned again towards each other.

It was Lord Corbury who first saw Fenella emerge from the bushes to stand there irresolute and uncertain.

"Good God!" he exclaimed. "What are you doing here, Fenella?"

To Fenella's consternation everyone turned their heads in her direction, and she knew by the expression in Sir Nicolas' face that he very much disapproved of her presence.

"I had to . . . see what . . . happened," she murmured in a low voice.

"What with Drury Lane Dramatics and a crowd of spectators we might as well be in Piccadilly," Lord Corbury remarked in disgust.

And then suddenly his sense of humour asserted itself.

"Blast it! But this is the most ridiculous duel in which I have ever taken part," he said and began to laugh.

Just for a moment it seemed as if Sir Nicolas's stiff attitude would not allow him to relax. Then he smiled too and putting up his pistol discharged it into the air.

"Honour is satisfied!" he said and he looked at Fenella as he spoke, knowing she would approve of his action.

Not to be outdone, Lord Corbury lifted his pistol and fired at the sky. Then he walked towards Sir Nicolas and held out his hand.

"I apologise, Waringham," he said. "I knew even as I said it that you would not allow any horse from your stable to be pulled."

It was a generous gesture, and Fenella looked at him with an expression of happiness which released the tension from which she had been suffering all night.

"Well, I will tell you one thing, Corbury," one of his seconds said, "this is the last time I creep out of bed with a splitting head to support you. There is not even a bleeding body to show for all my endeavours!"

"Nevertheless," one of the other Gentlemen remarked, "I am now cursed hungry having got up so early. What do you say if we all go to the Club for breakfast?"

"That is a most sensible suggestion," the Referee remarked.

"Good idea!" Lord Corbury agreed and looked at Sir Nicolas.

"I hope you will all honour me by being my guests," he said as if he knew it was expected of him.

Lord Corbury handed his pistol to one of his friends who placed it in the duelling-box.

"I will take Miss Lambert home," he said, "and join you within ten minutes."

As he spoke he took Fenella by the arm.

"Come along," he said. "I cannot think what the world is coming to when a man cannot enjoy the privacy of a duel without females poking their noses into it and making a thorough nuisance of themselves!"

He was however, Fenella knew, no longer angry and she detached herself for one moment from his side to give her hand to Sir Nicolas.

"Thank you," she said softly. "You know I am grateful."

He understood only too well what she meant. At the same time she saw the hurt in his eyes and knew he thought her gratitude was only because Periquine was saved from injury.

She wanted to reassure him by saying that she had worried about him too, but there was no time.

He raised her hand to his lips, and then Lord Corbury was taking her away through the trees to where his Phaeton was waiting.

A groom was holding his horses heads and after

Periquine had helped Fenella up into the seat and taken up the reins, they drove away alone through the trees towards Lord Farquhar's house.

"There is something I want to tell you, Fenella," Lord Corbury said.

"What is it?" she asked apprehensively.

There was something in his voice which told her that what he had to impart was serious.

"I am going to India."

"To India!" Fenella ejaculated.

Whatever she had thought to hear this was totally unexpected.

"I am leaving almost immediately. I was told by a friend of mine last night there are enormous opportunities there for any young man who will spend a few years learning about and handling the merchandise which is being shipped from the East to Europe in large quantities."

"How will you get . . . there? How can you . . . afford it?" Fenella gasped.

"I meant to borrow the money," Lord Corbury said, "but last night when I returned home I had a talk with your uncle and he has been exceedingly helpful. He has promised to give me an introduction to a number of firms who are already established in India, and he has also offered to pay my fare and give me enough to live on until I can find my own feet."

"But . . . Periquine, it is . . . so far . . . away," Fenella said almost childishly.

She thought she could not bear him to go! It would mean he would be away for years and she would not see him. What was more, she was quite certain that once he had left England he would forget her very existence.

For one second she played wildly with the idea of asking him to take her with him—as his wife— as his mistress—she did not care in which capacity she travelled as long as she was with him.

And then she knew that he would not want her

company. He would wish to be alone. He would not want the responsibility or the trouble of being hampered with a woman.

"It has great possibilities, I am sure of that," Lord Corbury was saying. "I cannot understand why I did not think of it before."

"How ... long ... do you think you will be ... away?" Fenella asked.

"Your uncle suggests that in four, perhaps five, years if I use my intelligence, I should be able to return with a fortune."

Four or five years! Fenella could not whisper the words even beneath her breath. Now before they could say more they had turned in at the drive of Lord Farquhar's house and the big red brick mansion loomed ahead of them.

"Surely we must ... talk about it ... decide what is ... best ..." she began wildly.

"I have made my decision," Lord Corbury affirmed. "I shall leave as soon as possible."

"But, Periquine ..." Fenella began and then realised there was nothing she could say.

He drew up his horses outside the door, and feeling as if she had been given the death sentence, Fenella put out her hand to a footman who had hurried down the steps to assist her.

Then as she alighted the Butler came to the side of the Phaeton.

"There is someone to see you, M'Lord," he said to Lord Corbury.

"At this hour of the morning?" Lord Corbury asked raising his eyebrows.

"Yes, M'Lord. Apparently he has urgent business with Your Lordship which took him to the Priory. When he found your Lordship had left for the races, he travelled here and arrived about half an hour ago. He is at this moment in the Salon with the Master."

Fenella had listened to this conversation with surprise.

"Fancy Uncle Roderick being up so early," she remarked to Lord Corbury.

He was climbing down from the Phaeton, and as he did not answer her the Butler said with a touch of rebuke in his voice:

"His Lordship is always up early, Miss. In fact His Lordship attributes his good health to the fact that he usually has a ride before breakfast."

The word breakfast seemed to remind Lord Corbury that he had an appointment with his friends.

"Keep the horses," he said to the Butler. "I cannot believe this stranger's business with me will take long."

He followed Fenella up the steps and across the hall towards the Salon.

A footman opened the door for them and Fenella entered to see her uncle in riding-breeches standing by the fire-place and beside him a small grey-haired little man, wearing neat sombre black garments which seemed instantly to proclaim him as being a clerk of some sort or another.

"Good morning, Fenella," Lord Farquhar said, "and good morning to you, Periquine. You appear to be in good shape."

There was a twinkle in his eye as he spoke and Lord Corbury answered briefly.

"The duel was concluded in a somewhat unexpected fashion."

"You are Lord Corbury?" the little man asked.

"I am."

"Then may I, M'Lord, introduce myself? My name is Salter and I'm the Senior Clerk to Mayberry Letchington and Mayberry, Solicitors to your late Uncle —Colonel Alexander Massingburg—Corbury."

There was a moment's pregnant silence. Then Lord Corbury said slowly:

"You said my late uncle?"

"It is with deep regret, M'Lord, that I have to inform you that the Colonel was mortally injured while out riding four days ago. His horse failed to clear a brick wall and in falling crushed your uncle beneath him so that he died almost immediately."

Lord Corbury said nothing, it seemed as if he

was turned to stone. Then as if he chose his words with care he said:

"You came down from Yorkshire especially to find me?"

"Yes, M'Lord," the Clerk replied. "Mr. Mayberry, the Senior Partner, asked me to inform Your Lordship not only of your Uncle's sad demise, but also that it is imperative for you to journey to Yorkshire as soon as it is humanly possible."

"You mean," Lord Corbury began.

"I mean, M'Lord, you are the sole beneficiary under your Uncle's Will. Mr. Mayberry requires your presence and your assistance, which is why he sent me South with instructions to find you."

"I understand," Lord Corbury said.

He had turned rather pale, Fenella thought, but otherwise his voice was quite expressionless as he said:

"Perhaps you would be good enough, Mr. Salter, to give me some idea of what my Uncle's estate comprises. I have not seen him for over five years."

"But of course, M'Lord," Mr. Salter answered, "although it is difficult to be accurate until things are wound up. There are large properties in Yorkshire, a mansion with quite a sizeable estate in Leicestershire and Corbury House which, as Your Lordship well knows, the Colonel took over from your late father in Grosvenor Square as well as some other properties in London."

"It sounds a considerable amount," Lord Corbury said, still in a low calm voice which Fenella knew meant he had complete control of himself.

"It is very difficult," the Clerk continued, "to give your Lordship more information until Mr. Mayberry has gone further into the details of your possessions. But he did mention to me just as I was leaving that, if Your Lordship should ask, he was certain that the money in the bank, and the shares owned by your Uncle in very reputable firms, would touch a figure of not less than half a million pounds!"

It was Fenella who gasped quite audibly. Lord

Corbury said nothing, but he could not prevent a sudden light showing in his eyes as he said quietly:

"Thank you for the information, Mr. Salter."

"I know, dear boy," Lord Farquhar interposed, "that you will wish to be on your way to Yorkshire immediately, I have therefore taken upon myself to lend you a four-in-hand. It will carry you more swiftly than your Phaeton, and you can change horses for the first time at my own stables in London."

"It is very obliging of you, M'Lord," Lord Corbury said. "And if you will excuse me I would of course wish to be on my way."

He looked at the Clerk.

"Will you travel with me, Mr. Salter?"

"I should be honoured, M'Lord."

"I shall have to stop for a few minutes at the Club and tell my friends that I cannot breakfast with them," Lord Corbury said, "though I will undoubtedly feel justified in partaking of a glass of wine."

His eyes met Lord Farquhar's as he spoke and the two men smiled at each other. Then Lord Corbury held out his hand.

"Thank you," he said, "for the kind offer you made me last night. Can I leave Fenella in your charge?"

"You can do that," Lord Farquhar said, "and the best of luck, my boy!"

"Thank you," Lord Corbury replied.

He turned towards Fenella. She was looking up at him beseechingly, her face very pale. He put his hand on her head and ruffled her hair.

"Take care of yourself, Imp," he said, "and do not get into any more mischief if you can help it."

Her hands fluttered out towards him, but already he had walked from the room swiftly and with an eagerness that he could not hide.

Fenella followed him. As she reached the hall she saw the four-in-hand was already waiting outside the front door and the servants lifting Lord Corbury's valise into it.

He swung himself onto the box-seat, Mr. Salter

scrambled up beside him and the groom seated himself behind.

The horses were fresh and fidgeting to be off. And it was with great difficulty that while keeping his leader under control, Lord Corbury managed to raise his hat as he drove away.

Fenella put up her hand and waved but he did not look back. She watched his broad shoulders and the raffish angle of his head until the drive turned and he was out of sight. Forlornly she let her arm fall down to her side.

"Half a million pounds!" she murmured almost beneath her breath. "Oh, Uncle Roderick, I have lost him now! He will be able to . . . marry Hetty as he has always wanted to do."

Lord Farquhar put an arm round her shoulders.

"You might do well to remember an adage from the racing world," he said. "It is—'One has never lost a race until another horse is first past the winning post'!"

Three weeks later, helping himself to cutlets furnished by his own lambs, garnished with mushrooms picked in his own meadows, Lord Corbury looked across the large oval room in which he was sitting through the high windows onto the well-kept garden, which was bathed in sunshine.

It was a fine day and he was thinking that he would rather ride across the fields to inspect the work that was taking place in one of his villages than drive round the twisting narrow lanes.

He was waited on at breakfast by an elderly Butler, who had the appearance of a bishop, and three footmen.

Another flunkey appeared to whisper something in the butler's ear, who now approached His Lordship respectfully to say in a low voice:

"I would inform Your Lordship that Mr. Tothill the architect is here to discuss with Your Lordship the plans for the new buildings on the West side of the Estate, and Wingate and his son who are concerned with the drainage of the land down by the river have been waiting Your Lordship's pleasure for nearly an hour."

"I will see them all in a few minutes," Lord Corbury replied. "Have you told my agent to be here at 9:30?"

"I sent a groom to Mr. Walker's house last night, M'Lord, after I received your instructions."

"Thank you, Barnstaple," Lord Corbury said, "There is a lot to do!"

He spoke with a note of satisfaction in his voice and the Butler replied:

"There is indeed, M'Lord. But if your Lordship will permit me to say so, as Mr. Walker was saying only yesterday, there has never been a gentleman who seemed to grasp the intricacies of the situation so quickly, who was so positive in deciding what should be done."

Lord Corbury permitted himself a smile of satisfaction.

It was true, he thought. He had never realised before what pleasure there was in planning an estate or setting in motion the architects, the builders, the stonemasons, the carpenters and all the other people who were vitally concerned with the projects he had in hand.

"I'm afraid," the Butler was saying, "that Your Lordship has found that the late Master was only concerned with the well-being of his horses. He had little interest in his tenants or indeed in the farming of his land."

"I must admit to being surprised at how much needs doing," Lord Corbury agreed.

He waved away two other dishes that were proffered him by the footmen.

"I have no time for more," he said. "Besides, I shall find myself putting on weight if the Chef continues to send up such excellent food at every meal."

"Adolphus will be very gratified, M'Lord," the Butler said, "to know his efforts have found favour in your eyes. He is indeed an artist at his work, but he gets very despondent if he is not appreciated."

"Then tell him I am extremely pleased with his efforts," Lord Corbury said.

He picked up a glass of ale by his side as he spoke. It was ale that had been brewed in his own brewery on his own estate, and which he felt, though it might have been imagination, was better than any other ale he had ever tasted in his whole life.

He was about to rise from the table, when a flunkey placed a silver salver in Barnstaple's hand.

He brought it to Lord Corbury's side. On the shining surface reposed two letters.

"The post has just arrived, M'Lord."

Lord Corbury picked up the letters. There was no mistaking on the first at which he looked that the elaborate, elegant script was the effort of a female and the other with its curling capitals was also from a woman.

A footman set a gold-handled ivory letter-opener at his Lordship's side and he slit the first letter open.

It was scented with gardenia, and as this was a perfume he had every reason to remember, he did not need to glance at the signature before he started to read.

10th July 1817

Periquine, my Very Dear,

    It is with the greatest Joy I have heard of your Good Fortune and of the vast Estates your Uncle has Bequeathed to You on his Death.

    As the London Season is over You will have Realised that we are now at Brighton where His Royal Highness the Prince Regent is in Residence. It is very Gay, but as You can Imagine I miss you Sadly.

    Please hurry South to join Us and Papa is greatly looking forward to Welcoming You.

    I remain, Dear Periquine,
        Yours ever Affectionate,
            Hetty

There was no mistaking the curl of contempt on Lord Corbury's lips as he read Hetty's letter. When he came to her reference to Sir Virgil he smiled, but there was no humour in it.

He threw the letter down on the table and picked up the other one. He knew the writing only too well. It was from Fenella and he read:

July 11th 1817

Dearest Periquine,

I feel very Remiss in not writing before to Condole with you on your Uncle's Death and express my deepest Sympathy for the Tragic manner in which He met it. Please forgive me, but I have been so exceedingly Busy these past weeks that I have hardly had time to Think.

You will no doubt see that I am writing to You from Brighton where Uncle Roderick has a most charming and spacious House on the Steine next to those owned by the Duke of Marlborough and Mrs. Fitzherbert.

Such Exciting things have happened to me since You left that I hardly know where to begin to tell You about them.

Uncle Roderick has appointed Himself my Guardian and has decided most generously to present me to the Fashionable World. He has given me the most beautiful gowns and you will be astonished, Periquine, to hear that I am a Success!

We go to Balls and Assemblies every night, and I have dined twice at the Royal Pavilion where His Royal Highness paid me the most fulsome Compliments and even placed Me on his left at Dinner!

I know you will tease me when you hear that several Suitors have asked Uncle Roderick if they may pay their Addresses to me!

*It is all very Exciting and sometimes I feel I
must be living in a Dream!!*
　　　*Take care of Yourself, dear Periquine.
We often speak of You.*
　　　　*Your affectionate cousin,
　　　　　Fenella*

Lord Corbury read this epistle through twice.
While he was frowning the first time, he was definitely scowling ferociously on a second reading.

For a moment he sat staring at Fenella's signature as if he had never seen it before.

Then he rose from the table so hastily that his
chair tipped over backwards and fell with a crash to
the ground, which made the attendant footmen step
forward hastily.

Crumbling Fenella's letter fiercely into a ball in
the palm of his hand, he walked from the room.

Chapter Ten

Lord Corbury drove into Brighton late in the afternoon, tooling his four horses with an expertise which made a number of people turn round and stare at him in admiration.

He had been agreeably surprised to find such a perfect team of chestnuts in the stables at Corbury House in Grosvenor Square, and knew that they would undoubtedly be the envy of his friends.

He drove up with a flourish to the best hotel on the Marine Parade and demanded a suite of rooms with such an authoritative air and was obviously of such consequence that the proprietor without a qualm of conscience handed over to him the rooms he had been keeping for the Earl of Dorchester.

Having changed his clothes, Lord Corbury proceeded to Lord Farquhar's house on the Steine and asked to see Miss Fenella Lambert.

He was however shown into a study on the ground floor, where he found himself greeted by Lord Farquhar.

"This is a surprise, Periquine, dear boy," the latter said jovially, "we were not expecting you South for some time."

"I wish to see Fenella," Lord Corbury said with the air of a man who is not to be diverted from his main objective.

"Fenella is resting at the moment," Lord Far-

179

quhar replied. "We are dining tonight with the Prince Regent at the Royal Pavilion, and naturally she wishes to look her best."

"When can I see her?" Lord Corbury demanded.

"Sit down, my boy, and let me offer you a glass of wine," Lord Farquhar said. "We have heard very pleasing reports of the possessions and the fortune you have inherited from your uncle. I feel sure they are not exaggerated."

"Not in the slightest," Lord Corbury replied, "but there is a great deal to do. I have started a programme of rebuilding a number of the villages on my Yorkshire estates, which at a rough estimate will keep me fully occupied for the next five years."

"That is good news," Lord Farquhar approved. "As I expect you know, your Uncle acquired his Yorkshire estates from his first wife who was a great heiress. His second brought him the lands in Leicestershire."

"I had forgotten that Uncle Alexander was married twice," Lord Corbury said. "I think his second wife died before I was very old."

"You cannot have been more than five years of age," Lord Farquhar agreed, "and after that the Colonel found being a bachelor suited him admirably. With his wealth I can assure you he was never lonely!"

"I can well believe that," Lord Corbury smiled. "And now will you tell me when I can see Fenella."

There was a moment's pause. Then Lord Farquhar said:

"Fenella is being a great success, Periquine. I always realised she was very attractive, but I can assure you that with her looks, her charm and that *joie de vivre* which makes her outstanding among young women, she has taken the *Beau Monde* by storm."

Lord Corbury did not speak but his lips tightened as Lord Farquhar continued:

"I do not mind telling you, Periquine, that I am besieged by prospective suitors, and I think we shall be very proud of our little Fenella before the end of the week."

"What do you mean by that, My Lord?" Lord Corbury asked sharply.

"I mean," Lord Farquhar replied slowly, "that I expect Fenella to make a brilliant match—very brilliant indeed."

Again there was a silence, and then in a voice which sounded unnaturally loud Lord Corbury asked:

"Is it Waringham?"

"Good Heavens, no!" Lord Farquhar replied. "Fenella had refused Sir Nicolas I understand, before you stayed with me at Ascot. But he is still exceedingly persistent. At times I cannot help feeling sorry for him."

"Refused him!" Lord Corbury murmured almost as if he spoke to himself. "I might have suspicioned it."

"No, it is not Waringham," Lord Farquhar went on, "but someone of far greater consequence in the social sphere. Tonight, as I have already told you, dear boy, we dine with His Royal Highness. But tomorrow the Dowager Marchioness of Harrington is giving a Ball for her daughter at which Fenella will be an honoured guest. I should not be surprised if the announcement of Fenella's engagement to the young Marquis was made during the ball."

"I insist on seeing Fenella," Lord Corbury said sharply. "If she is lying down I can go up to her room. After all I am her cousin, or she can come down here to me."

Lord Farquhar rose from the arm-chair on which he had been sitting to stand in front of the fire-place. He did not look at Lord Corbury, but he appeared to be choosing his words carefully when he said:

"Now, Periquine, we both, as I well know, have Fenella's interests at heart. I have no wish for you to come barging in at this particular moment perhaps making trouble. Childhood sweethearts and all that sort of thing often unsettle a young girl when she is making a decision on anything so important as marriage. What I would like to suggest is that you go to the Priory or anywhere else you fancy, but stay away from Brighton for the next forty-eight hours."

"Why should I do that?" Lord Corbury asked truculently.

"Because I think it is in Fenella's best interest," Lord Farquhar replied.

Lord Corbury rose from the chair in which he had been sitting to walk restlessly across the room towards the window.

Having reached it he stared with unseeing eyes at the blue sea, his chin set in a manner which Fenella would have recognised as a sign that he was at his most obstinate.

He stood still for quite a minute before he turned round to say:

"I presume that as Fenella's Guardian you would consider it correct that I should ask you if I can pay my addresses to her?"

Lord Farquhar stared at him in what appeared to be genuine astonishment.

"Pay your addresses to Fenella!" he exclaimed. "But, my dear boy, the whole of Brighton is expecting you to marry Hetty Baldwyn! Sir Virgil has been telling all his most intimate friends that the engagement will be announced as soon as you come South."

"Let me make this quite clear," Lord Corbury retorted, "I do not intend to offer for Hetty Baldwyn or for any woman other than Fenella!"

"Good gracious me," Lord Farquhar said. "I quite understood that you were infatuated with the other young woman, and it was only your lack of fortune that was keeping you apart."

Lord Corbury had the grace to look slightly shame-faced.

"I admit to having found Miss Baldwyn extremely attractive for a short while," he said. "She is undoubtedly a very beautiful girl. But when I came to know her character better and realised that her pretty head would always undoubtedly rule the vacillations of her heart, I was no longer interested."

"You have certainly surprised me," Lord Farquhar ejaculated. "So now at this somewhat belated hour you have transferred your affections to our little Fenella? Well, Periquine, as far as I am concerned I forbid you, absolutely and categorically, to approach Fenella or to make her an offer of marriage!"

He paused before he added:

"As I have already told you, I have very different plans for her, which I am sure would meet the approval of the most ambitious Mama who ever launched a débutante upon the social world."

He walked across the room to put a hand on Lord Corbury's shoulder.

"I do not suppose your heart is seriously involved, dear boy, and I can assure you that now you are so warm in the pocket you will find any number of attractive young women only too ready to throw themselves without even a momentary hesitation into your manly arms."

He added with a smile:

"What is more, if you take my advice, you will take your time in choosing one. There is nothing so amusing, or indeed so flattering, as being a matrimonial *parti*, as I have found all through my life."

Lord Corbury did not answer. For a moment he glared at Lord Farquhar with a ferocious frown upon his forehead and then without a word he turned and went from the study slamming the door behind him.

Lord Farquhar went to the window to watch him drive away and as he did so the door opened and Fenella came in.

She was looking extremely attractive in a négligée of oyster silk trimmed with lace, and her deep red hair, which had not yet received the ministrations of a hair-dresser, was hanging over her shoulders.

She ran towards Lord Farquhar, her eyes wide and curious.

"He has gone!" she exclaimed. "What did he say? Oh tell me, Uncle Roderick, I could hardly bear not to come down and see him!"

"He has left in a rage that was quite intimidat-

ing," Lord Farquhar replied with a smile. "After I
had told him of my plans, he asked if he could pay
his addresses to you."

Fenella clasped her hands together.

"Uncle Roderick, is that the truth? You are not
teasing me?"

"No, I assure you, the words almost seemed to
blister his mouth, he was so incensed."

Fenella threw her arms round Lord Farquhar's
neck and kissed his cheek.

"I cannot believe it is true!" she cried. "Do you
really think he cares for me?"

"I am quite certain he does," Lord Farquhar
said. "As I told you when you were so unhappy,
there are some people who cannot see the wood for
the trees. It is only now that Periquine is afraid of
losing you he realises how much you mean to him."

Fenella took her arms from her Uncle's neck and
put her hands against her breast as if to still a tumult
raging there.

"Do you believe it was my letter which has
brought him South? Hetty is proclaiming to the whole
of Brighton that she had written to him and that she is
expecting him to come to her side post-haste."

"I think Miss Baldwyn is in for a shock," Lord
Farquhar said, "and I must say it will give me great
pleasure to circumvent the greedy advances that Sir
Virgil has undoubtedly been making in Periquine's
direction. He would have given him short shrift when
he was a pauper."

"He would . . . indeed."

Fenella spoke in a low voice and then she said:

"I cannot really . . . credit that Periquine . . .
cares for me as much as he cared for . . . Hetty."

"That is why," Lord Farquhar said briskly, "you
are to behave exactly as we agreed. No weakening,
Fenella! Remember your whole happiness for the
future depends on your being sure in the very depths
of your heart that Periquine loves you."

Fenella sighed.

"I will do what you have told me to do, Uncle

Roderick," she said meekly. "After all perhaps it was
the letter we concocted with such pains which has in-
cited him to travel here from Yorkshire, and not
Hetty's soft persuasiveness."

"I am quite certain," Lord Farquhar said, "that
we will have to play young Periquine with the skill
one would expend on catching a salmon."

Fenella was still for a moment and then she said
hesitatingly.

"You do not think it . . . wrong, Uncle Roderick,
to . . . behave in this manner? I would not wish him
in the future to feel he was . . . caught."

"Wrong?" Lord Farquhar questioned. "I can remember my brother telling me he was not interested
in women and concerned only with books. Then a
very pretty girl with eyes like yours was continually
begging him to translate the Latin names of flowers
and plants in which she was interested, until one day
my brother forgot his books and found that a pair of
green eyes were considerably more beguiling."

"So that was how Mama managed to marry
Papa!" Fenella cried. "And actually, Uncle Roderick,
her Latin is just as good if not better than his."

"But of course!" Lord Farquhar agreed. "Most
men, my dear Fenella, have to be persuaded or shall
we say tempted into marriage. After all there are so
many advantages in being free to pick and choose."

Fenella gave a little sigh.

"I want to be sure . . . quite sure . . . that
Periquine really . . . loves me," she whispered.

Dressing for the Dowager Marchioness of Harrington's Ball the following night, Fenella felt so miserable it was hard to take any interest in her appearance.

Even a new gown of white satin, trimmed with
lace so fine that it might have been made with fairy
fingers, failed to bring a smile to her lips.

She had done exactly what her uncle had told
her the previous evening, and now she thought his
advice had been disastrous.

Lord Corbury had arrived at the Royal Pavilion after dinner with a number of other guests invited by the Prince Regent.

Fenella had seen him enter the exotic Chinese Salon and heard his Royal Highness greeting the young man for whom he had a warm affection.

But she had pretended not to notice, and made a valiant effort to concentrate on what the Marquis of Harrington, Sir Nicolas and Lord Worcester were saying to her.

Finishing his conversation with his host, Lord Corbury had looked round for Fenella and seen her at the far end of the room laughing gaily at something one of her escorts had said.

The smile faded from his lips and there was a frown between his eyes as he started to move through the throng of distinguished personages to her side.

Before he had proceeded far a voice cried:

"Periquine!" and a hand went out to touch his arm.

He looked down to see Hetty, exquisite in a pale blue gown which matched her eyes, her hair the soft gold of ripening corn, her red lips pouting up at him in a provocative manner.

"I heard that you had arrived in Brighton," she said softly, "and I was expecting to see you earlier this afternoon."

"Your pardon, Hetty," Lord Corbury said, "but I have to speak with Fenella."

To the Beauty's astonishment, he moved swiftly away from her side to leave her staring after him in perplexity.

Directly avoiding a number of people who wished to engage him in conversation, Lord Corbury reached Fenella and she turned towards him with a cry of delight:

"Periquine! What a surprise!" she exclaimed. "I had no idea you were coming to Brighton."

She was looking, Lord Corbury noticed with no particular pleasure, very different from when he had last seen her.

Her dark red hair skilfully arranged in the latest fashion framed her small face from which he noticed the freckles had vanished, and her skin, which had not been noticeable in her old faded gowns, was very white and lovely against the dress of apple-green gauze which sparkled with every movement she made.

Lord Corbury had not realised in the past what an exquisite figure Fenella had.

Now with the new tight waist which had been reintroduced into fashion and her small breasts clearly defined by her well cut gown, it was obvious that she was indeed perfectly proportioned.

"When did you arrive?" Fenella was asking, "and how have you enjoyed yourself in Yorkshire?"

"I want to tell you all about it," Lord Corbury said in a deep voice.

"Of course, I wish to hear every detail," Fenella answered, "but at the moment I am afraid I am engaged for the next dance."

"Which is mine," the Marquis said firmly.

Fenella smiled at him.

"I had not forgotten," she said her eyes meeting his.

"And the next is promised to me," Sir Nicolas interposed.

Fenella made a little gesture with her hands.

"I dare not disappoint these gentlemen, Periquine."

"No indeed," Lord Worcester said, "we have all a prior claim! And I can assure you, Corbury, we will unite to prevent any bumping and boring on your part!"

The Gentlemen laughed at this, but Fenella saw Lord Corbury's lips tighten.

As she moved towards the Ball Room on the Marquis's arm, she glanced back to see him looking after her and, if she had not been sure that her uncle's advice was right, she would have run to his side to tell him he could dance with her whenever he desired to do so!

Now she wished she had done just that, because Lord Corbury had left the Royal Pavilion early and although she had expected him to call on her the next morning, he had not appeared at Lord Farquhar's house then or later in the day.

"Could he really be put off so easily?" Fenella asked herself. "If so, he cannot really . . . love me."

Her love for him was like a continual ache in her heart.

However gay she might appear, however much of a success she might have been these last three weeks, she had gone to bed every night thinking of Periquine, longing for him and knowing that the emotions he evoked in her were so deep, so overwhelming, that every day the hurt of them grew worse.

"I love him . . . I love him . . ." she whispered into her pillow.

When the dawn broke, she would wish only that she could be back at the Priory in her old gowns tidying Periquine's room, ironing his cravats, and slaving after him as she had done ever since they had been children together.

At the same time her success in the Fashionable World had given her a sense of self-confidence that she had never had before and a pride which made her realise that Periquine's love must be as deep as her own or they would never know true happiness.

She had listened to him eulogising about Hetty. Was it possible that he would ever feel the same about her?

It was a question that remained unanswered in her mind all day.

When the hours passed so slowly that each one seemed like a century and there was still no sign of Periquine, she knew a darkness and despair which encompassed her like a thick fog.

"He loves you," Lord Farquhar had said consolingly just before Fenella went up to change for dinner.

"Then he has a . . . strange way of . . . showing it," she sighed.

"Perhaps he will turn up at the Ball tonight," Lord Farquhar suggested.

"I hope . . . so," Fenella murmured miserably.

Her maid wished her to lie down, but she felt so depressed that she knew it would be worse lying in the darkness thinking about Periquine than being able to move about.

The hair-dresser came early to do her hair as he had a large number of other ladies to attend to in succession, and when he had gone Fenella put on her new gown. She thought as she did so it was far the most becoming of all those Lord Farquhar had bought for her.

There was a string of pearls to fasten round her neck and there was also a diamond brooch to wear in front of her decolletage.

She looked at it in the glass and wanted only that Periquine should see her.

Once when she had worn his mother's green gown, he had told her that it made her skin look white. The pearls and tiny diamonds which ornamented the lace on the bodice, gave her skin a kind of translucence which few other girls had.

It was due, she knew, to her red hair, and she wanted Periquine to realise that now at last she was not so afraid of the contrast between herself and Hetty.

Why did he not come and see her?

She had asked herself this question a thousand times during the day and now she went to the window to see the sun sinking low in the sky and wondered if the night would bring an eclipse of all her hopes and desires.

There was a knock on her bed-room door.

"The carriage is here, Miss, and His Lordship says as the horses are fresh will you come down immediately."

"So early!" Fenella exclaimed.

Nevertheless she picked up her wrap of satin edged with swansdown and followed the footman down the stairs.

It was unlike her uncle, she thought, to wish to arrive early at the dinner party they were attending before the dance.

Then she remembered that the Dowager Marchioness's house was not in Brighton, but a little way outside. It would be impolite to be late and she was certain Lord Farquhar, who was punctilious over such matters, would have timed their arrival to a nicety.

The footman was moving swiftly ahead of her, almost too swiftly for decorum, and Fenella remembered that he was a new recruit to the staff. The old butler, who had been with Lord Farquhar for some years, had already made several complaints about him suspecting he took tips from importunate guests.

There was no-one in the hall which again surprised Fenella because there was always a Butler and two footmen in attendance to see His Lordship into his carriage.

The footman pulled open the door and outside Fenella saw not the large formal carriage which her uncle usually used in the evening with his coat-of-arms emblazoned on the door, but a very smart D'orsay Curricle, a new vehicle which had recently come into fashion and which Fenella knew was noted for its speed.

The hood was up and although her uncle often tooled his own horses, she was surprised he should do so at night.

Then she thought that the Dowager Marchioness's house must be further from Brighton than she had first imagined.

The groom was holding open the door of the curricle and he helped her up the step. As she bent her head to move under the hood into the seat beside the driver, Fenella exclaimed:

"I have never been with you in a D'orsay Curricle before, Uncle Roderick, in fact I did not know you had one."

She sat down as she spoke, and with rather a bump as the horses sprang forward. Then she looked at the driver whom she supposed to be her Uncle and saw it was Lord Corbury.

"Periquine!" she exclaimed. "What are you doing here and where are you taking me?"

She was aware even as she spoke that behind the hood and obscured from sight the groom had swung himself into an upright seat.

But to all intents and purposes she was alone with Lord Corbury and she looked at him a little apprehensively wondering what this action on his part could possibly mean.

Then with a little sinking of her heart she saw that his chin was squared and his mouth set in a hard line.

She knew him too well not to recognise the signs if not of rage, certainly of some irritation that invariably preluded an uncomfortable argument or perhaps a row.

She drew in her breath and as she did so she realised that the horses were moving unusually fast.

Then as they turned off the Marine Parade, she was aware that Periquine was driving at a breathtaking speed which could in fact be dangerous.

The horses were certainly fresh and although there were only a pair of them, the Curricle was very light and soon its wheels hardly seemed to touch the ground, they were moving so swiftly.

"What is happening? Please explain, Periquine! Did you arrange with Uncle Roderick to take me to the Ball? He did not tell me you intended to do so."

"I have nothing to say to you until we reach our destination," Lord Corbury replied.

His voice sounded hard and harsh and Fenella looked at him in perplexity.

"How handsome he is," she thought.

She felt her heart turn over in her breast because she was close to him and because her love for him made her feel curiously weak.

In fact she could not think clearly as to what was happening or why Periquine was behaving in this unaccountable manner.

They drove on and on and she knew that Periquine was forcing an almost abnormal pace out of his horses.

She recognised the road, which she had driven over often enough, and now she was certain they were long past the house where the Ball was to take place and were on their way towards the Priory.

"Why," she asked herself, "why was Periquine taking her away from Brighton, and what had he to say to her that he could not have said in her uncle's house or anywhere else that they might have met?"

She was however too afraid of the grim determination on his face and the tightness of his lips to venture any more questions.

Besides it was quite hard at the pace they were travelling to keep her balance and she was concentrating on holding onto the side of the carriage so as to prevent herself from being thrown against him.

They could have only driven for perhaps twenty minutes when the journey usually took thirty-five or forty, when she saw ahead of them the gates leading into the Priory.

"So I was right," she thought to herself, "that is where Periquine is taking me."

She could not help feeling a little glow of happiness at the thought that whatever he might have to say he wanted them to be together in his home.

Then to her complete astonishment they passed the Priory, and even as Fenella looked round with enquiry in her eyes, Periquine turned his horses off the road and onto a cart track which led into the woods.

He was forced to slow his pace as dusk was falling and it was not so easy to see the way. But to Fenella it was as familiar as every path in her own garden.

She opened her lips to exclaim and to question Periquine once again as to what he was doing.

Then before she could speak she saw ahead of them the little Church-in-the-Woods and Periquine drew his horses to a standstill outside the door.

She turned then to ask the question trembling on her lips, but he avoided her glance and getting out of the Curricle walked round to assist her to alight.

The groom was already at the horses' heads and a gesture from Lord Corbury made him take them a little further on, so that he was out of earshot.

"What are we here for?" Fenella asked at last.

Her voice was tremulous, partly from the speed at which they had travelled and the shaking she had received in the process.

"I have brought you here to marry you," Lord Corbury replied.

"To ... marry me!" Fenella exclaimed.

"You are mine!" he replied. "You have always been mine, and if you think I am going to allow you to marry anyone else, you are very much mistaken! You will agree to marry me here, now at this moment, Fenella, or I will make you."

She felt her heart leap, but because she was curious she could not help asking.

"How ... will you ... make me?"

There was still a darkness in Periquine's eyes as he looked down into her face.

"It will not be difficult," he said slowly. "You are very small and I have always been able to compel you to do anything I wished, but alternatively I could take you into the woods and ravish you. Then you would feel obliged to marry me."

"Periquine!" Fenella gasped, "are you really saying such things to me?"

"I do not intend to argue with you, Fenella," he said. "Will you marry me willingly or do I have to make you obey me?"

Fenella's heart was beating frantically. At the same time she felt a wild elation sweeping over her, and in a voice which trembled, but not entirely from fear, she said softly:

"I will ... marry you, Periquine."

He offered her his arm in a manner which she felt was half ironic and then as she put her fingers on

it, he led her through the open door of the Church
and into the aisle.

It was very dim inside, for the trees excluded the
day-light, but the candles were lit on the Altar and
standing waiting for them was the old Rector.

Their footsteps seemed to ring out on the stone
floor as they walked towards him, and Fenella remembered how hiding in the Crypt they had listened
to the soldiers stamping overhead.

Then as she recalled Periquine's kiss and the
ecstasy she had known before she had become unconscious, she felt herself thrill again with an incredible rapture and which made her involuntarily
tighten her fingers on his arm.

They had reached the old Rector, and as he
smiled at them Fenella knew nothing would give him
more pleasure than to marry two people for whom he
had a fondness since they were children.

The marriage service began, and as Fenella listened to the beautiful words that were joining her to
the man she had loved so deeply ever since she could
remember, she was conscious of the soft scufflings of
small animals behind them, the flutter of wings in the
rafters.

She felt as if she was encompassed about with a
crowd of tiny witnesses who were a part not only of
the woods but of the Priory itself.

Lord Corbury drew a ring from the pocket of his
waistcoat and when the Rector had blessed it he put
it on to Fenella's finger saying:

"With this ring I thee wed, with my body I
thee worship, with all my worldly goods I thee en-
dow."

His voice was very deep and sincere.

Fenella felt as if her cup of happiness was filled
to the brim and flowing over, because now at last she
was what she had always wanted to be—Periquine's
wife!

They knelt. The old Rector blessed them and
they walked together down the aisle.

Without a word Periquine handed Fenella into

the Curricle climbed in on the other side and picked up the reins.

They drove off, Fenella acutely conscious of the ring on her third finger and the Rector's words when he had joined them together as man and wife echoing in her ears.

It was a very short distance to the Priory and Lord Corbury drew his horses up outside the front door which was open.

Again he helped Fenella to alight and as they walked up the steps and into the Hall she saw all the candles were lit but there was no-one about.

She stood irresolute looking up at him as he placed his hat and gloves on a table and came slowly towards her.

"There is food and drink waiting for us in the Dining-Room," he said and she thought his voice sounded entirely impersonal. "I told the servants to go to bed as we had no need of them tonight."

Then he looked down into Fenella's worried eyes and suddenly the expression on his face changed.

"You are mine, Fenella!" he said, "mine, and my wife as I always meant you to be! Oh my darling, my wonderful little love, how could you think of anyone else, how could you try and leave me when I need you so?"

He pulled her roughly into his arms and held her crushingly against him. As instinctively she lifted her face to his he cried:

"Mine! Mine! Mine!" and his voice seemed to ring out round the panelled walls.

Then his lips were on hers and Fenella felt the rapture that she had known once before shoot through her body like a meteor.

It made her feel that Periquine swept her away into a golden world where they were alone—and everything else was forgotten.

His arms tightened, his lips became more possessive, more passionate until she felt as if he drew her very heart from her body.

She was unable to move, unable to think! She

could only feel a wonder and a glory such as she had
never known existed.

Then with his lips on hers Periquine lifted her in
his arms and carried her up the stairs.

The candles which Mrs. Buckle had left alight
on one side of the bed gave as they guttered low
very little light through the heavy embroidered curtains of the big four poster bed.

There was a small fire in the grate because even
in the summer, unless the house was regularly occupied, it could strike cold.

Fenella stirred against Periquine's shoulder and
said softly:

"What can Uncle Roderick have thought when
he found I had disappeared?"

"I have no idea," Periquine replied, "and quite
frankly it does not particularly interest me. What is
important is—have I made you happy?"

"So . . . very . . . happy," Fenella whispered.

"And you love me?"

"You know . . . I . . . do!"

"Tell me—I want to hear you say it."

It was a command.

"I . . . love . . . you."

"My precious—my adorable little wife!"

His hands were touching her and she quivered
and thrilled until her breath came quickly between
her lips.

Perequine gave a little laugh and pulled her even
closer against him.

"I did not know that a woman could be so soft, so
sweet, so utterly and completely enchanting," he
said gently.

Fenella buried her face in his shoulder. When he
spoke to her in such a manner, her happiness was
almost too overwhelming to be borne.

"What made you spirit me away in such a . . .
manner?" she asked after a moment.

"I was afraid," Periquine replied, "afraid of losing you. I do not think I have ever suffered such

agonies as I did on the journey down from Yorkshire thinking I might be too late."

Fenella made a little murmer.

"You can never escape me now," he went on in a deep voice. "You are mine, my dearest Heart, mine as you always have been, only I was such a fool I did not realise it. You were so much a part of the Priory, my life and of me, that it was only when I thought that I might lose you I knew it was impossible to live without you."

"When did you first . . . know you . . . loved me," Fenella asked as every woman has asked since the beginning of time.

"When I kissed you in the Crypt," he answered. "As my lips met yours, I knew a magic I had never known before. I was aware then that you were what I had been looking for, you were what I had been seeking, and I had had no idea of it."

"It was . . . wonderful for me . . . too," she whispered, "but why did you not tell me that you . . . loved me?"

"Because I realised I had nothing to offer you," he answered. "How could I marry you knowing that the only way I could get money was to involve you in crazy dangerous adventures in which you might have been harmed. It had not mattered where other women were concerned, with you it was different."

He paused for a moment and then he said:

"That was why I was going to India to make money for you, my darling one. To work so that we could live together at the Priory."

He held her so tightly that she could hardly breathe as he said:

"How could I have been such a muttonhead as not to anticipate that you might find someone else when I was away? I just expected you to wait for me. I knew that we belonged to each other and I thought you must know it too."

"I do belong to . . . you. I always . . . have."

"You belong to me now," he said. "And you can

be sure of one thing, my precious, I will never let you go, never, never."

"As if . . . I would . . . wish to leave . . . you!"

"And I will not have you flirting with Waringham or anyone else," he said masterfully. "Let me make one thing very clear, Fenella, I shall be a very jealous husband."

He kissed her forehead as he spoke sweeping away her hair.

"I swear I will make you so happy that no other man will interest you."

Then he added:

"One thing I have done, which I think will please you, is that I have told Isaac Goldstein to vacate his house. I do not want him and his sharp methods in the Priory grounds."

"I am glad . . . so glad," Fenella cried.

"And I have told Joe Jarvis to buy his dogs at any price he wishes to ask for them. They can guard the Priory when we are not there, but I doubt if they will be much use when you pet and overfeed them."

"How wonderful of you."

"What is more a week ago I sent that damned Usurer £6000 anonymously."

He kissed Fenella's hair.

"We start our marriage with clean hands, my Sweetheart."

"I want . . . us to do . . . that," Fenella told him.

Then when he would have kissed her again she said:

"It may sound . . . unromantic, Periquine, but I am very . . . hungry. I could not eat any luncheon today and you did say there was some food downstairs."

He laughed.

"I am hungry too. When I came over here this morning to make arrangements for our wedding, Mrs. Buckle was not expecting me, and the only thing she could rustle up at a moment's notice was some ham and eggs! But she promised us a cold collation for this evening."

"That sounds delicious," Fenella smiled.

"I cannot wait for you to try the food which Adolphus my Chef in Yorkshire produces," Periquine said. "He is really superlative! And I hear my Chef in London is nearly as good."

He kissed Fenella's cheek, his lips lingering on the softness of her skin and said:

"Darling, darling, there are so many wonderful and exciting things to do together. Are you quite sure you love me?"

"I am absolutely . . . sure."

"Then let us go downstairs and find something to eat."

Fenella gave a little chuckle.

"You will have to find me something to wear. In your hurry to abduct me you omitted to provide me with any . . . night attire."

"I will bring you a robe."

Periquine got out of bed and went from the room to his dressing-room.

Fenella lay back against the pillows. She had never thought that she would lie in this bed with Periquine or be his wife.

How often she had tidied the room for him, how often she had cared for his clothes. Now she was his, as she had always wanted to be. It was like a wonderful dream!

He came back into the room wearing a long robe and carrying over his arm another made of soft green wool which Fenella recognised as one he had worn when he was at Eton.

She knew she could wrap it round herself and it would not be so overwhelmingly large as those he had acquired after he was grown up.

She sat up in bed holding the sheet over her breasts.

"That will do perfectly" she said, "give it me and turn your back."

He came towards her. Then as he reached the bed he looked down at her and suddenly walked to the other side of the room to stand with his back to

the fire-place. As he did so he threw the robe he held
in his hand down on a chair.

"Come here," he said.

Fenella looked at him in surprise. She was certain of the reason for his change of mood or why his
voice sounded suddenly hard.

"Come here," Periquine repeated. "You have just
promised to obey me, Fenella, and I expect you to
do so."

"But, Periquine," she protested, "I am . . . n . . .
naked."

"I like you naked," he answered. "Do as you are
told."

She hesitated for a second before bending sideways she blew out the two lights on the bedside
table. Then she slipped out of bed and ran towards
him and there was only the flames from the fire to
throw its soft lights on her white body.

She would have flung herself in his arms had he
not put out his hands and gripped her shoulders to
hold her at arms length.

She felt the colour rising in her cheeks as he said
firmly with an unflixable note in his voice:

"I love you, I adore you, I worship you, but I
will never, Fenella, and this is important, I will never
again take orders from a woman. Do you understand?"

She felt herself quiver and thrill because he was
so masterful.

This is how she had always wanted him to be,
positive, authoritative, sure of himself and very much
a man.

Then he swept her into his arms and his lips
were on hers.

She was utterly captive and helpless, beneath the
fierce insistence and the passionate demand of his kiss.

Until as the rapture and glory of their desire
carried them away once more into a secret world
where nothing else could encroach, Periquine picked
Fenella up in his arms and carried her back to the
bed.

ABOUT THE AUTHOR

BARBARA CARTLAND, the celebrated romantic author, historian, playwright, lecturer, political speaker and television personality, has now written over 150 books. Miss Cartland has had a number of historical books published and several biographical ones, including that of her brother, Major Ronald Cartland, who was the first Member of Parliament to be killed in the War. This book had a Foreword by Sir Winston Churchill.

In private life, Barbara Cartland, who is a Dame of the Order of St. John of Jerusalem, has fought for better conditions and salaries for Midwives and Nurses. As President of the Royal College of Midwives (Hertfordshire Branch), she has been invested with the first Badge of Office ever given in Great Britain, which was subscribed to by the Midwives themselves. She has also championed the cause for old people and founded the first Romany Gypsy Camp in the world.

Barbara Cartland is deeply interested in Vitamin Therapy and is President of the British National Association for Health.